"Being a self-employed industrial psychologi... perks, such as being flown around by a gorgeous charter pilot. Not that I'm interested in anything more than pleasant conversation. Experience has taught me that a delectable-looking package can camouflage a treacherous soul. Still, there's no harm in looking. And looking I am."
—Dr. Hope Hunt

"She was classy, business sexy. That was my first impression. But I knew Dr. Hope Hunt remembered my past. Most people related to NASCAR do. I prefer to avoid those who believe I have a tarnished reputation, but I don't have the luxury of turning down business."
—Brent Sanford

"My sister says Brent has gotten under her skin. With all the rumors flying around the track, I just hope she knows what she's getting into."
—Grace Hunt Winters

"My brother is innocent. He would never resort to sabotage, not in the past and certainly not now. That detective is wrong. There is no connection between Brent and the death of Alan Cargill."
—Adam Sanford

MAGGIE PRICE

A former police crime analyst for the Oklahoma City Police Department, Maggie Price has never tried to distance herself from her dark "cop side" to write the riveting romantic suspense that has become her trademark. If anything, that meshing of the cop and the romantic is a natural blending…and her stories show us that sometimes love can kill.

The riveting authenticity of police work and the sizzling passion she brings to her novels have earned her numerous awards, including a Golden Heart, a National Readers' Choice Award, a Bookseller's Best Award and a coveted RITA® Award nomination. Other honors received include an *RT Book Reviews* Career Achievement Award for series romantic suspense, and its Reviewer's Choice Award for "Best Silhouette Intimate Moments."

NASCAR®

BANKING ON HOPE

Maggie Price

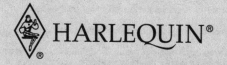

HARLEQUIN®

TORONTO • NEW YORK • LONDON
AMSTERDAM • PARIS • SYDNEY • HAMBURG
STOCKHOLM • ATHENS • TOKYO • MILAN • MADRID
PRAGUE • WARSAW • BUDAPEST • AUCKLAND

Recycling programs
for this product may
not exist in your area.

ISBN-13: 978-0-373-18530-6

BANKING ON HOPE

Copyright © 2009 by Harlequin Books S.A.

Maggie Price is acknowledged as the author of this work.

NASCAR® and the NASCAR Library Collection® are registered trademarks of the National Association for Stock Car Auto Racing, Inc.

www.eHarlequin.com

Printed in U.S.A.

To heroes who make our hearts race.

NASCAR HIDDEN LEGACIES

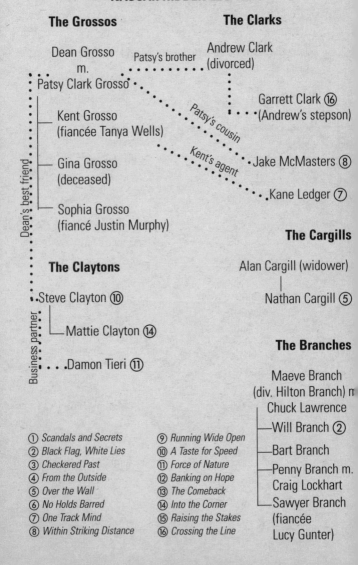

The Grossos

Dean Grosso
m.
Patsy Clark Grosso

Patsy's brother

— Kent Grosso
(fiancée Tanya Wells)

— Gina Grosso
(deceased)

— Sophia Grosso
(fiancé Justin Murphy)

The Clarks

Andrew Clark
(divorced)

Garrett Clark ⑯
(Andrew's stepson)

Patsy's cousin

Kent's agent

Jake McMasters ⑧

Kane Ledger ⑦

The Cargills

Alan Cargill (widower)

|

Nathan Cargill ⑤

Dean's best friend

The Claytons

Steve Clayton ⑩

— Mattie Clayton ⑭

Damon Tieri ⑪

Business partner

The Branches

Maeve Branch
(div. Hilton Branch) m
Chuck Lawrence

— Will Branch ②

— Bart Branch

— Penny Branch m.
Craig Lockhart

— Sawyer Branch
(fiancée
Lucy Gunter)

① *Scandals and Secrets*
② *Black Flag, White Lies*
③ *Checkered Past*
④ *From the Outside*
⑤ *Over the Wall*
⑥ *No Holds Barred*
⑦ *One Track Mind*
⑧ *Within Striking Distance*
⑨ *Running Wide Open*
⑩ *A Taste for Speed*
⑪ *Force of Nature*
⑫ *Banking on Hope*
⑬ *The Comeback*
⑭ *Into the Corner*
⑮ *Raising the Stakes*
⑯ *Crossing the Line*

THE FAMILIES AND THE CONNECTIONS

The Sanfords

Bobby Sanford
(deceased)
m.
Kath Sanford

— Adam Sanford ①

— Brent Sanford ⑫

— Trey Sanford ⑨

The Hunts

Dan Hunt
m.
Linda (Willard) Hunt
(deceased)

— Ethan Hunt ⑥

— Jared Hunt ⑮

— Hope Hunt ⑫

— Grace Hunt Winters ⑯
(widow of Todd Winters)

The Mathesons

Brady Matheson
(widower)
(fiancée Julie-Anne Blake)

— Chad Matheson ③

— Zack Matheson ⑬

— Trent Matheson
(fiancée Kelly Greenwood)

The Daltons

Buddy Dalton
m.
Shirley Dalton

— Mallory Dalton ④

— Tara Dalton ①

— Emma-Lee Dalton

CHAPTER ONE

BEING A SELF-EMPLOYED industrial psychologist had its perks, Dr. Hope Hunt thought as she wheeled her suitcase onto the tarmac of a small Dallas airport. Her latest consulting job was in her hometown of Charlotte where her family lived. Another advantage was that her client there—Sanford Racing—had chartered a private plane to fly her to and from its corporate headquarters.

Hope's eyes widened when she caught sight of the tall, lean, very-interesting-looking-from-the-backside pilot checking the single engine airplane parked beyond the chain-link fence. He wore black slacks and a crisply ironed, pale blue dress shirt that gave his powerful body an aura of brisk efficiency. Sunlight glinted off his thick brown hair. As he made his way around the plane, she noted he moved with the sinuous tread of a big cat. Pursing her lips, Hope decided the awesome view was just one more perk to add to the list.

Not that she was interested in anything more than some pleasant conversation with the man who'd be at the plane's controls. Experience had taught her that a delectable-looking package could camouflage a treacherous soul. Still, there was no harm in looking. And looking she was.

Which is why her throat snapped shut the instant he

turned to inspect the tip of one of the wings and she got a good look at his face.

Her newest client, Adam Sanford, hadn't mentioned he planned to send his brother, the notorious babe magnet and disgraced former NASCAR driver, to pick her up!

There'd been a time when Brent Sanford showed up regularly on sports broadcasts and eligible bachelor lists. That was before the scandal, which had ended his racing career.

Watching him, Hope's eyes narrowed while she gave herself a moment to evaluate the situation that faced her. In her job, she analyzed problems using compassion and a sense of fairness, meaning she was well versed in finding the silver lining in any dark cloud. So she scoured her memory while she trained her gaze over Sanford's clear-cut profile, studying the hard geometry of his jaw, the no-nonsense curve of his mouth. The bad-boy black-lensed sunglasses he wore just added to his total appeal. Bottom line, the man looked like the kind of fantasy a woman didn't want to wake up from.

But Hope was wide-awake and now operating in analytical psychologist mode. In Sanford's defense, he had earned an entirely different reputation as a top-notch pilot who'd made a stunning success of the air charter service he started after his racing career tanked. She knew all too well how much hard work and forti-tude it took to establish—and operate—a successful business. If for no other reason, she could credit the man for proficiency in his current endeavor.

Tightening her fingers on the handle of her suitcase, she squared her shoulders. The plane he was examin-ing was a two-seater—no way could she fly for hours beside him while acting as if she considered him a low-life cheat. She'd been born with the gift of gab, a skill she'd refined over the years, so she would be polite to Brent Sanford and keep her personal opinion of him to herself. No reason things shouldn't run smoothly during their flight, she told herself as she headed across the tarmac.

THE SOUND OF HIGH HEELS clicking against asphalt had Brent turning. He recognized the brunette heading his way on the opposite side of the chain-link fence from the picture he'd seen on her Web site. She wore a tailored black suit on her slim, tight frame. The skirt stopped just above the knees and was slit on one side, showing off what seemed like a mile of leg. *Great-looking legs.* She pulled a suitcase behind her with one hand while she carried a slim leather briefcase in the other.

Business sexy.

A pair of black designer-looking sunglasses camouflaged her eyes, which he remembered from her picture were a smoky-gray. Her dark hair was board straight, the blunt-cut locks clipped to just about chin level. When he opened the gate in the fence and got a closer look at her, he thought: classy. She had God-given perfect bone structure. Her skin was lightly tanned, her lips colored in rich peach.

Although that mouth was curved up at the corners, the stiff set of her shoulders made him suspect that Dr. Hope Hunt recognized him and knew all about his past. No surprise there. Almost everyone in her family had some sort of connection to NASCAR, so it would have taken a major miracle for his current fare not to have heard about his notorious past.

Which was something he'd known the instant his brother asked him to fly Hope Hunt while she was under contract to Sanford Racing. Considering his tarnished reputation, he'd have preferred to have the option of avoiding anyone with even the vaguest ties to racing and, more specifically, to NASCAR. But he had busted his butt to build Sanford Aviation from the ground up. He owned two planes outright, and had just doubled up on payments on his pride and joy, a six-seater Lear. He had rent, salaries and other expenses to pay, so he didn't have the option of turning down business. Even if it meant staying on the edges of the profession in which most people considered him a liar and a cheat.

Good thing he'd long ago accepted the hand fate had dealt him and resolved not to let what other people thought of him matter. If the classy brunette about to climb into his plane considered him lower than slime, so be it.

When she reached the open gate, she held out her hand. "Captain Sanford, I'm Hope Hunt."

He lifted a brow as his hand encompassed hers. "Nice to meet you, Dr. Hunt. Why don't you call me Brent?"

HOPE ALMOST FALTERED at the firmness in his grip. His fingers were strong, his skin rougher than those of the business executives with whom she usually associated. The heat that seemed to zigzag between their palms made her heart lurch.

She was so dismayed by her reaction, she barely registered his question. "Uh, Brent it is. I'm Hope." She suspected he'd felt the sensation, too. Why else would his hand linger on hers a moment longer than necessary?

He nodded toward her suitcase. "Let me take that for you."

She watched him heft her bag into the luggage area behind the plane's front seats, then he turned and gave her high heels a pointed look. "I'd better help you into the plane."

"All right."

His hold on her elbow was as equally strong as it had been on her hand. As she belted herself into the copilot's seat, she noted her heart was still beating too fast.

How pitiful was it that she would respond so easily to the simple touch of a man's hand? Not just any man, either, but one who epitomized the same morally bankrupt personality traits of the snake who'd broken her heart to bits.

She watched as he started the engine, adjusted controls. "Flying…Charlotte…be…less…three…."

"What?" she asked over the engine's loud drone.

He retrieved the copilot's headset, handed it to her and motioned for her to put it on.

"We'll be in the air about three hours," he said. "Feel free to read, take a nap."

She shook her head. "I don't mind flying in small planes, but I never relax enough to do either," she responded into the microphone.

"Unfortunately, Sanford Aviation doesn't show in-flight movies." He reached into a compartment on the door beside him and pulled out a small bag. His mouth quirked up on one side. "But we do offer peanuts and bottled water to our guests."

Even over the headphones she heard the dryness that had settled into his voice. She would give the man points for having a sense of humor.

"Thanks," she said and accepted the bag.

As they taxied toward the runway, her gaze lingered on his hands, so sure and steady on the controls. Those same hands had steered race cars to heart-stopping finishes. She had even been in the stands and witnessed some of those races. He had won them fair and square. The psychologist in her would love to delve into his mind and find out what had motivated him to cheat to try to win that last race.

Mulling that over, she busied herself with opening the bag of nuts while he conversed with the controller in the tower.

Soon, the plane lifted into the air, as smooth as silk.

So far, so good, she thought and tilted the bag his way. "Want some?"

BRENT SLID HER A SIDEWAYS look, his gaze stopping on her hand gripping the bag. Her fingers were long and slender, her nails polished a petal-pale. When he'd shaken that hand, he'd found it soft and small, but firm enough. He was still trying to figure out what the heck the sensation was that he'd felt running up his arm the instant flesh had met flesh. "No thanks."

A psychologist, he thought as he took in her profile. She looked as if she should be leading cheers at a varsity game. Or sipping some high-dollar brandy at a ritzy hotel. He wasn't certain why both images seemed to suit her, but they did. It was the image of a doctor that didn't. Weren't psychologists supposed to be staid and wrinkled and sit in a dusty office while probing into people's minds? Or was that a psychiatrist? And what the heck was the difference between the two professions?

"Something wrong?" she asked.

"No." He flicked his gaze back to the controls. And because she'd caught him studying her, he added, "Your brother is a crew chief for one of Sanford Racing's teams. I see the resemblance."

"Since we have the same father but different mothers, does that mean you're implying I have a five o'clock shadow and unruly hair like Ethan?"

THE GRIN BRENT FLASHED put a slow, liquid tug in Hope's belly. Instantly, an alarm blasted in her head. Oh, no. No, no, no! The last time she'd felt *that* sensation she'd wound up engaged to a two-faced creep whose secret passion had been scamming rich Texas widows. Brent Sanford might be a prime piece of eye candy, but she'd rather be boiled in oil than have anything to do with another man who saw nothing wrong with cheating to get what he wanted.

"I should have said I see a *family* resemblance between you and Ethan," he said. "Same mouth shape. Similar jawline. Facial hair doesn't come into play."

Lord, even his voice sounded suddenly softer coming over her headphones. The quivering sensation in her stomach deepened, making her feel vulnerable and exposed.

Her fingers clenched on the bag of nuts and she could almost feel a sense of self-preservation surge inside of her, along with a ripple of panic. So much for being polite. She needed to erect a wall, and the quickest way to do that was to let Brent Sanford know she was aware of exactly what kind of person he was.

"I guess you know my other brother Jared, too," she said. "And my dad. He was crew chief for Cargill Motors for years."

"I've met them."

She noted the muscle that had gone tight in Brent's jaw. Not a surprise—it had been a Cargill-owned car at the center of the scandal that ended his racing career.

"I used to have more time to go to the track," Hope added. "So, I've seen you race. The last time," she added pointedly, "was at Talladega."

MESSAGE RECEIVED, LOUD and clear, Brent thought. Talladega had been where his career had unraveled. For some reason, the good doctor had decided he needed to know she'd witnessed the entire fiasco in person.

Fine. Dandy.

He reached down, retrieved a map and as good as shoved it into her hand. "Do me a favor and check our location."

Hope blinked. "You don't know?" She waved a hand toward the dash. "Isn't that a GPS screen?"

"It is. But I use it more for backup." He inclined his head. "Check out the window for towns, lakes, railroad tracks, highways. Anything that can be used as a point of reference. Then find it on the map."

Despite her sunglasses, he could see her eyes had narrowed. "Do you require everyone who flies with you to navigate?"

"No." Just the ones who bring up my past, Brent thought, then banked the plane into a turn.

BY THE TIME THEY LANDED in Charlotte and walked into the fixed base operator's service facility, the tugs on Hope's conscience were sharp and impatient. Her job was all about looking for reasons, causes, then to treat. Not to judge. It had always been a matter of pride that she had the ability to put personal emotions aside when dealing with clients, and anyone else, for that matter.

That had so not been the case with Captain Handsome. The only excuse she could come up with for taking a swipe at Brent Sanford was that his too-charming-for-his-own-good grin had shocked her libido out of the hibernation it had been in for the past two years.

Apparently she was attracted to men of low moral fiber. This time, though, she knew the type of land mines that could be hidden behind a compelling grin. She had no intention of walking onto that type of danger zone again.

"Brent! Glad you're back." A blonde with vivid blue eyes and a slight Southern drawl motioned to him from behind the customer service counter. She was tall and slim and wore a sleeveless blouse that showed off tanned, well-toned arms.

He acknowledged the woman with a nod, then looked at Hope. "I need to drop some paperwork by my office." He pulled off his sunglasses and anchored one earpiece in the pocket of his starched blue shirt. She discovered that his eyes were so deeply brown it was impossible to see a boundary between pupil and iris. "That won't take long," he added. "Then I'll drive you to my brother's office."

"You don't have to do that. I grew up here, so I know my way around. I can rent a car."

"My brother asked me to drive you to Sanford Racing. I told him I would." He raised a shoulder. "Believe it or not, I keep my word."

Ouch. The swipe she'd taken at him had definite' hit the target. Hope's conscience pinged a little If she let him drive her, she could use the o to apologize.

"All right, then." She swept a hand tow

able-looking sofa and chairs near a grouping of vending machines. "I'll wait there."

She watched him walk toward the counter, noting again the economy of movement in his gait. Even so, she sensed a restlessness in him. It was difficult not to appreciate the way he held it in check.

When he reached the counter, he opened the leather satchel he'd carried in from the plane and pulled out a small package wrapped in gold and topped with a red bow.

The blonde beamed a smile when he handed her the gift. Then she leaned across the counter and pressed a kiss to his cheek.

Well, Hope thought. The man who'd been rumored to have numerous women at his beck and call apparently hadn't altered that aspect of his life.

The blonde gripped his forearm, put her head back and laughed at something he said. Hope imagined that by now, Brent Sanford's blood was pumping just a few beats faster.

Easing out a breath, she tried not to wonder why that thought didn't sit well.

HOPE WASN'T SURPRISED WHEN she discovered the pilot/former NASCAR driver owned a black, sleek foreign car that looked as if it belonged in a cage. After all, he used to make his living by going fast. But if she'd expected they would zoom through Charlotte's heavy traffic like a heat-seeking missile while hard rock screamed from the radio, she'd have been sorely disappointed.

Brent Sanford drove like a responsible citizen—keeping the speed low and even, accelerating gradu-lly and easing off the gas at intersections. The radio was set on a station that played earthy, mellow blues. Even so, by the time he pulled the car into Sanford Racing's parking lot, the highway that had been outrageously jammed with bumper-to-bumper traffic had her gritting her teeth.

He, on the other hand, looked as if they'd just taken a relaxing drive in the country.

"This is it," he said, inclining his head in the direction of the three-story cream-colored stucco building with windows tinted a smoky-gray. Tidy flowerbeds that bloomed in vivid colors bordered the front of the building.

"Once you get inside, the elevator is just to the right," he added. "Adam's office is on the second floor."

"You're not coming in?"

"This is as far as I go." He checked his watch. "I have another charter for early evening, so I have to get back to the airport."

She'd waited as long as she could to say what she needed to say. "Before you leave, I'd like to apologize."

He eased a shoulder against the driver's door while resting one wrist over the top of the steering wheel. "For?"

"What I said in the plane. About my . . . ng you race at Talladega. I brought that up so . . . now what I was there when the scandal broke . . . over to open her door.

"Yeah, I got that." He . . . sper of a touch, but Hope Their bodies brushe was, determined not to let him refused to a . . . wouldn't have brought it up."

She . . . d you?"

She . . . ed her eyes for an instant. No way was . . . sb admit that the effect he'd had on her ho . . . made her panic and toss up the first wall . . .

to mind. "How about I just say I'm sorry and leave it at that?"

He regarded her for a long moment, his dark glasses camouflaging his eyes. "Sounds to me like the head doctor prefers to ask questions instead of answer them."

She relaxed enough to smile. "I have to admit it's easier to ask than to answer."

"A hell of a lot easier. Which makes me glad I'm not on the list of people whose heads my brother has hired you to look into."

"Actually, my expertise is team building. I spend more time observing how people interact than I do trying to figure out what's in each individual's head."

"You ever get accused of invading someone's privacy?"

She always made an effort to meet cynicism with humor. "Once, when I walked in on my brother Ethan and his girlfriend while they were making out on the living room couch."

Her dry tone apparently got through, making his lips twitch. "Your point, Doctor." He rechecked his watch. "I need to make a couple of stops on my way back to the airp—"

She knew a hint when she heard one. "And I've held you up long en—

As she slid out—

While he lifted her s— car, he climbed out on the other side.

studied his profile that wa— out of the trunk, she lid. He looked safe, solid, th— highlighted the planes and angles o— by the trunk got a glimpse of a man whom a wom— n a woman feel safe with. —unlight —— she

Hope shook off the thought. She'd made a policy not to analyze people who hadn't signed up for it. Still, she was curious. So while he slid the handle up on her suitcase, she asked, "If your name were on Adam's list, what would I find by getting a look into your head? All sorts of unresolved issues?"

"Nope. Everything about me is tied up in a neat package." He shut the trunk with a decided snap, then turned to face her. "I don't need fixing."

"That's fortunate."

"I'll say."

She offered him her hand. "Thanks for the smooth flight, Captain."

"My pleasure, Doc."

When his fingers locked on hers, the tension snapped into her again, the ripe man-woman connection she hadn't felt with anyone in years, until a few hours ago. This one man who looked so good on the outside, and was everything she detested on the inside, was making a joke of her self-control.

She slid her hand from his, forced herself to take an emotional step back.

She in no way intended to do anything about the kick his touch put in her blood. Still, the devilish tickle of temptation that had started the second he touched her bare skin still tingled through her fingers.

As she watched him drive away in his sleek, black car, she decided it might be a good thing that Tall, Dark and Handsome was headed back to the airport and on his way out of town.

CHAPTER TWO

AT THE SAME INSTANT HOPE wheeled her suitcase into
the lobby of Sanford Racing headquarters, a tall, strap-
ping man with dark hair and laser-blue eyes stepped off
of the elevator.

"Ethan!"

Grinning, her half brother strode toward her across
the tiled floor. Dressed in a team polo shirt and dark
pants, Ethan Hunt wrapped a rock-hard arm around her
waist and caught her in a hug. "How's it going, Brat?"

His use of the childhood nickname he'd stuck her
with had Hope jabbing a playful finger into the exact
spot on his ribs where she knew he was most vulnerable.
"Things are fine and dandy."

He winced while rubbing his side. "Man, you don't
ever change, do you?"

She beamed him a bright smile. "Why mess with perfection?"

Turning, she noted the unattended receptionist's desk
while peering around the lobby lined with glass cases
and shelves that held trophies, photographs and other
racing memorabilia. A pristine race car sat on the far
side of the lobby. Its hood was raised to display an
engine that gleamed like newly polished silver.

"Are you my official greeter?" Hope asked.

"More like unofficial. I was upstairs in Adam's office when his brother called to tell him you were on your way in." Ethan shrugged. "I think Adam was hoping Brent would escort you to his office, but since that didn't happen, I volunteered to come down and meet you."

She glanced back toward the lobby's entrance. When she'd stood in the parking lot beside Brent, there'd been a moment after he slipped off his sunglasses and looked toward the building. An emotion she'd been at a loss to name had flickered in his eyes. *Maybe regret*, she thought now. While he was a driver for his family's business, his entire world had no doubt revolved around this building and the sport of racing. Getting caught sabotaging a competitor's race car had cost him dearly.

"Anyway," Ethan said, drawing her attention back. "Right after Brent called, the owner of Greenstone Garden Centers walked into Adam's office."

"I take it the owner is important?"

"Slightly. Greenstone is the major sponsor for Sanford's NASCAR Sprint Cup Series car. I told Adam I'd give you the fifty-cent tour of the facility while he's tied up. We can stash your suitcase upstairs with his secretary, then head down to the garage area."

"You lead, I'll follow."

Furrowing his brow, Ethan put a finger under her chin, nudged it up and studied her face. "You know what, Brat? Each time I see you, you get prettier."

"Yeah? You, too." *And happier*, she thought. When his wife died suddenly four years ago, Ethan had been devastated. With grief surrounding him like a force field, he'd allowed their daughter to move in with his in-laws and closed himself off emotionally. Now, though, eleven-year-old Sadie was back home with her father and Ethan was engaged to a woman named Cassie Connors. Hope had never met Cassie, but she'd received high praise from every member of the family. Seeing a spark in her big brother's eyes after so long warmed her heart.

"So, your fiancée works here, right?"

Ethan nodded while commandeering the handle of her suitcase. "Cassie's office would have been our first stop on the tour, but she's at the dentist. Her sister works here as a mechanic, so you'll get to meet Mia at least."

"Sounds like you're surrounded by Connors."

Ethan grinned. "It's a good feeling."

"That's obvious," Hope said, marveling at how happy he seemed after so many years of sorrow. "When do I get to see my niece?"

"Tonight. Sadie and I are having dinner at Dad's. Grace has a catering gig, so her kids will be there, too."

"Super," Hope said. One drawback to living in Dallas was that she only got to see her nieces and nephew a few times a year. "So, how's the crew chief business?"

"I had a rocky time a few months back. Now that you're onboard, I'm hoping things with the team will improve."

His suddenly serious tone stirred Hope's curiosity. "What things?"

"I'll let the boss cover that with you." Ethan slid her a sideways look while they headed toward the elevator. "Before Adam hired you, he asked me if I thought we'd be able to work together."

"Since I'm here, you must have said yes."

"I did. But it was damn hard keeping quiet over how you used to pout when all of us played games and you didn't get your way."

"I never pouted. I *sulked*."

He swung an arm around her shoulders. "Whatever you say, Brat."

She delivered a second poke to his ribs. "According to Grace, you and Jared gave me that nickname the day Mom and Dad brought me home from the hospital. There was no way I deserved it."

"Sure there was. You cried a lot. All that noise interfered with our routines. Then when you got older, you kept badgering us to play with you."

She fluttered her lashes. "Nothing wrong with that."

"We were teenagers by then. You wanted us to haul you along on our dates. Total bratty behavior. Even Grace agreed with us."

Hope pursed her mouth. Ethan and Jared's mother had died when they were young. Years later, their father married a widow who had a daughter, Grace. Husband and wife adopted each other's children, then together had Hope. The Hunt family had been a not-all-related-by-blood loving mishmash.

While they waited for the elevator, Hope nodded toward the shiny race car positioned under spotlights. "I take it somebody won a major race driving that?"

"Only the NASCAR championship," Ethan said drily. "That jewel of a race car belonged to Wild Bobby Sanford. He founded Sanford Racing."

"Was he?"

"Was he what?"

"Wild?"

"Oh, yeah. On the track and off." The elevator door slid open. Ethan waited until she stepped inside to follow her on. "He was an amazing driver who believed in testing the rules every time he raced. He's been dead ten years and he still holds the NASCAR record for the most

times being suspended from racing. He was also a notorious womanizer. Did a poor job of keeping his extracur-
ricular activities a secret from his wife and three sons."

Brent being one of those sons, Hope thought. Apparently where women were concerned, the apple hadn't
fallen far from the tree.

"In fact," Ethan continued, "Wild Bobby died of a heart
attack while on a deep-sea fishing trip with his mistress."

"Ooh, that's not good."

"An understatement. The boat's captain was a race
fan and knew that the woman wasn't Wild Bobby's
wife. The captain tipped off a sports reporter."

Hope furrowed her brow. "How come I never heard
about that?"

"Let's see, you'd have been fifteen years old then.
You were head cheerleader, dating the star quarterback
and president of the honor society. You didn't have time
to pay attention to anything that happened outside of
your busy universe."

"Good reason." Before the elevator door slid shut,
she took another look at the shiny race car. The psychologist in her felt an innate curiosity about what
dynamics had been involved in the Sanford family
while Wild Bobby was alive.

"Dad said you're bunking at his place while you're
working this job."

Ethan's comment pulled Hope's gaze back to his.
"Yes. You, Jared and Grace all assure me Dad's doing
fine on his own. He tells me that, too, whenever we talk."

Ethan stabbed a button on the elevator's control
panel. "Don't you believe us?"

"He and Mom were so close. And the cancer took her
so fast." Hope pulled in a deep breath against the instant

tightness in her chest. The grief
mother sometimes still washed
whenever she spoke to her fath
heard a sadness in his voice that

"I guess I just need to see for n
ling things."

"Mom died less than a year ago, quietly. "Take it from me, the only thing that'll help Dad recover is the passage of time."

Reaching out, Hope squeezed her brother's hand. As a widower, Ethan knew about loss all too well.

"In the meantime," he continued, "Dad's keeping busy. He watches Grace's kids when she has a nighttime catering job. Sadie hangs out at his place, too, sometimes. Believe me, all those grandkids keep him on his toes."

"Which is a blessing," Hope said.

Still, she couldn't shake the memory of the pain she heard so often in her father's voice.

So much for her curiosity about the dynamics of the Sanford family, she thought. While she was in Charlotte, she needed to concentrate on her own family.

THOUGHTS OF HOPE HUNT STILL weighed on Brent's mind an hour later as he nosed his sports car into its allotted slot outside the airport's fixed base operator's private terminal. Crossing the parking lot, he let himself in the door on the side of the building, swiping his ID card to unlock it.

While striding down the brightly lit hallway, he pictured how she had looked, sitting in the copilot's seat of his plane, then later in his car, dressed in her trim business suit, gazing at him through those big designer sunglasses.

...ke most everyone on the planet, she believed ...s guilty of sabotaging a competitor's race car.

He had no clue what had motivated her to suddenly toss the scandal in his face. Or the reason she'd later apologized.

Dr. Hunt, he thought, was a piece of work.

As far as he was concerned, his brother's insistence on hiring a psychologist to analyze why the overall performance of one of Sanford Racing's pit crews seemed flawed was a waste of money and time. They seemed to be doing fine. But Adam was in charge of the business, and when it came to what went on at Sanford Racing he called the shots. He wanted perfection.

Brent knew there was no way in hell he would ever agree to let Dr. Hope Hunt analyze what was in his head. Even if she smelled like sin and had the best legs he'd laid eyes on in years.

He frowned over that last thought. *That* kind of thinking had seemingly gotten him in trouble, he reminded himself as he paused just outside the door to his office. He took a deep breath while memories of what had occurred four years ago at Talladega seeped in, unpleasant, stirring, bombarding him with mixed emotions.

When NASCAR officials discovered a foreign substance in the gas tank of Kent Grosso's race car, everyone assumed someone on Grosso's pit crew had tweaked the fuel in order to give them an edge against the competition. That had been partially true—Mike Jones, a gas man on Grosso's crew had readily confessed he *had* spiked the fuel. But all hell broke loose when Jones claimed he'd been bribed by a driver for another team to add the supposedly untraceable compound to the gas that would damage the car's engine.

When Jones named *him* as the driver who'd done the bribing, Brent had thought he'd stumbled into a nightmare.

But he'd been wide awake, and things had only gotten worse when surveillance tape surfaced of him and Jones talking at a bar two nights before the race. Cash deposited the following morning in Jones's bank account gave further credence to the man's claim he'd accepted a bribe.

Brent's sole hint as to why Jones set him up came when he slugged the bastard and he'd rasped, "I did it for *her*."

Because of his father's exploits—and the pain the philandering had caused his mother—Brent had always been careful to be up-front about wanting no strings or emotional entanglements. But Jones's apparent motive had prompted him to take a hard look at the long chain of women whose lives he had come and gone from in a blur. Now, four years later, he still couldn't pinpoint any one female who'd had reason to set him up to take the fall for sabotaging a competitor's car.

And with Mike Jones having as good as disappeared off the face of the earth, Brent doubted he would ever find out what woman the former gas man had thought needed avenging.

Brent paused in the hallway outside of a door that displayed Sanford Aviation in bold, black letters.

Flying had always been a hobby. Racing his dream. When he walked away from NASCAR, his hobby had saved him. He'd put the brakes on his freewheeling lifestyle and focused all of his time, energy and money into parlaying his piloting skills into building a successful air charter operation.

Sometimes, the realization of how the life he'd mapped out for himself had changed in a heartbeat almost overwhelmed him. Before the scandal, he wouldn't have let a woman like Hope Hunt walk away without first getting her phone number. These days, though, he was gun-shy when it came to the fairer sex. Moreover, there was a stigma attached to his name, and any woman worth her salt wouldn't want anything to do with a man who was a known cheat.

He didn't blame them. Still, none of that made him want any less.

He rolled his shoulders in an effort to loosen some of the tenseness that had settled there. He hadn't been looking forward to the upcoming flight to New York, but now he was glad his evening was booked. Otherwise, he'd spend the time thinking about Hope Hunt.

Shoving open the door to his office, he stepped into the small reception area where Maureen "Mo" Queen sat industriously tapping away on her computer keyboard. Fresh flowers bloomed in a vase on her desk, the fragrance mingling with that of coffee. His office manager looked like a grandmother with her smoothly brushed gray hair and high-necked blouses, but she ruled their little kingdom with an iron fist and a total lack of tolerance for slackers.

"I was hoping I'd make it back before you left for the day," he said.

"I'm putting the finishing touches on a letter," she said, glancing up over the top of her monitor. "I checked with the FBO, they've got the Cessna SkyCatcher washed and refueled, so it's ready to take off for New York when you are."

"Great. All I need now is for the client to show up."

"Speaking of clients, a man called earlier wanting to book a flight first thing in the morning to L.A. Since you won't be back from New York, I phoned Randall and scheduled him to make the L.A. run." Randall Paris was one of two part-time pilots on call to take charters when Brent was flying elsewhere.

"What would I do without you, Mo?"

"Flounder," she said succinctly. "I've written up the contract sheets on the New York and L.A. flights. They're on your desk."

"Super."

Just then the door swung open. Brent turned, saw a medium-height man with brown hair step inside. Dressed in jeans and a black golf shirt, he had the strap of a leather briefcase looped over one shoulder and carried what looked like a bakery cake box in the crook of one arm.

"Help you?" Mo asked.

"I'm Tony Winters. I've got a flight chartered to New York."

Brent stepped forward, offered his hand. "I'm Brent Sanford, Mr. Winters. I'll be flying you. We should be able to take off on time."

"Great." Winters paused. "I don't know if anybody's hungry, but I've got a box of hors d'oeuvres here."

Mo leaned forward in her chair, her chin raised as if she were sniffing the air. "Where did you get a box of hors d'oeuvres?"

"My sister-in-law owns a catering company. I had to stop by her place on my way here to drop off some paperwork. She has a gig tonight, so she had all the ovens fired up. She shoved this box into my hands and told me to enjoy my dinner." He handed the box to Mo. "Since I wasn't headed home, I thought I'd see if anyone here wanted to indulge."

Mo's eyes went wide when she saw the logo on the top of the box. "*Gourmet by Grace?* Your sister-in-law is Grace Hunt Winters?"

"The one and only."

"Oh, my gosh." Mo flipped open the lid and reached inside. "I never miss watching her show."

"She has a show?" Brent asked. His mind had focused on the caterer's middle name. He recalled that Grace Hunt Winters had once been the personal chef for a NASCAR driver. She was also Hope Hunt's sister. So much for having this upcoming flight divert his mind from the doctor.

Mo handed him a pastry-wrapped hors d'oeuvre. "Boss, don't you ever watch TV?"

"Sports. News. Not cooking shows." He took a bite of the pastry. Inside was a pâté seasoned with what he thought might be a hint of fresh thyme. All he knew for sure was that he'd just had a taste of heaven. "This is awesome."

Winters beamed a smile. "That describes everything Grace cooks."

"She has a NASCAR cookbook coming out soon," Mo said around bites. "I've already got my copy on order." She pushed her chair back and rose. "I'm going to get myself a cup of coffee. Either of you want one?"

After both men declined, Mo scurried away, nibbling on an hors d'oeuvre.

Brent gestured toward one of the vacant chairs on the far side of the reception area. "Mr. Winters, you can wait here while I call and check with the weather service. Then we can head out to the plane."

"One thing I need to mention."

"What's that?"

"This trip to New York. I'm going there for a job interview. I've already got a position here with Matheson Racing and I help Grace out with her company's books."

"Go on," Brent prompted when Winters hesitated.

"The interview's just preliminary and I don't want anyone to know I might be headed to greener pastures. Grace mentioned that her sister, Hope, was doing some work for Sanford Racing and was flying in today on a charter. I checked around and found out you're the one who flew her in from Dallas."

Brent wasn't surprised Winters knew Adam had hired Hope Hunt. News and gossip often spread faster than a rocket blasting off. "That's right."

"If you wind up flying Hope again, I'd appreciate it if you didn't mention my trip. She might say something to Grace about it, and Grace would get upset, thinking I was for sure leaving town. Since nothing might come of this interview, there's no reason for her to know yet."

"Not a problem," Brent said before plucking another hors d'oeuvre from the box. "You have my word I'll keep this trip to myself."

Winters nodded. "Thanks."

Brent turned and headed for his office. Just giving his word seemed good enough for Winters. Somewhere in the back of his mind Brent suspected that Hope Hunt wouldn't trust him enough to take him at his word on any issue.

He'd spent the past four years convincing himself that what other people thought about him didn't matter. For some reason, she seemed to be an exception.

"So, Ethan gave you the full tour?" Adam Sanford asked after he and Hope settled into the conversation pit across from his desk. Even with his suit jacket off, shirt collar unbuttoned, sleeves rolled up and tie loosened, the man who controlled Sanford Racing exuded authority.

He was six-foot-something tall, with broad shoulders and lean hips. His dark hair was cut just a little shorter than his pilot brother's. Although his eyes were green instead of brown, it was easy to see the family resemblance between Adam and Brent. And their younger brother, Trey, whose pictures Hope had seen in the lobby's trophy cases.

She'd also spotted a few photos of Wild Bobby Sanford. Clearly, the three sons had inherited the "unbelievably handsome" gene from their notorious father.

"Ethan showed me every nook and cranny in this building," she confirmed. "We toured the fabrication shop, the engine building area and the garage. Even the gift shop." She sipped the tea Adam's secretary had delivered in a china cup emblazoned with the Sanford Racing crest. "All very impressive."

"Thanks." He sampled the coffee he'd opted for. "Running two cars this season keeps everyone on their toes."

"You run one car in each series, right?"

"Correct. Shelly Green drives our NASCAR Nationwide Series car. My brother Trey represents Sanford Racing in the Sprint Cup Series." Adam paused. "Did Ethan explain to you that because of a medical procedure, Trey sat out the last race?"

"He mentioned it."

"Same goes for the upcoming one in Richmond. While Trey's sidelined, Shelly is driving his car."

"She must be a good driver."

"Came in third in last week's race in Atlanta." Adam smiled. "She's snagged her own sponsorship deal, too. I plan to give her a full-time NASCAR Sprint Cup ride next season."

"So, you'll be running two cars in the Sprint Cup Series?"

"Not until next year. After Shelly drives in Richmond, she'll go back to the Nationwide Series."

"It sounds like there's no problem with Shelly's driving. Has Trey's health affected how he performs on the track?"

"It did for a time, but his driving is improving. Meeting a woman who's now his fiancée has made a world of difference for Trey."

Hope kept her expression benign. Adam had mentioned his own fiancée earlier. Plus, Trey Sanford was engaged and so was her brother Ethan. She hoped all three men had better luck with their intended spouse than she'd had with the quick-to-flatter louse she'd nearly married.

Switching her mind back to business, she settled her teacup on the table beside her chair. "It doesn't sound as if you hired me as a team builder because of either Shelly's or Trey's driving."

"I didn't." Adam set his coffee mug on an end table. "You live in Dallas, so NASCAR news—especially tabloid-type news—isn't as big there as it is here. Have you heard anything about Trey's trips to Mexico?"

Hope furrowed her brow. "Seems like I saw an article about him being involved with a woman there."

"If what I'm about to tell you were to be made public, it has the potential to create a media firestorm, and not in a good way. That's why I inserted a confidentiality clause in the contract I sent you."

"Even if you hadn't I treat all information regarding my clients' business as confidential. That's a strict policy of mine that every member of my staff understands."

"All right." Adam leaned forward, resting his elbows on his knees. "It's true that Trey's involved with a woman in Mexico, but it isn't a romantic relationship. She's an American doctor whom our dad first took Trey to when he was sixteen. He'd sustained a head injury—totally unrelated to his racing—and his doctor here discovered he has a mild form of epilepsy."

"Epilepsy?" The surprise that jolted through Hope sounded in her voice. "What about seizures? Isn't it dangerous for him to be driving at all, much less in NASCAR races?"

"That's everyone's initial reaction. And the reason Dad took Trey to Mexico. Even then it was clear Trey could become a great race driver, so Dad didn't want to risk that by having Trey stigmatized by having epilepsy."

"But, if he could have a seizure at any time…."

Hope let her voice trail off when Adam lifted a hand. "That's just it, Trey hasn't had a seizure in six years. The type of epilepsy he suffers from is almost undetectable and involves no loss of consciousness because the seizures are more like a few moments of daydreaming. People with this form of epilepsy sometimes don't even realize they have it until it's discovered during some other medical treatment."

"So, if Trey hadn't sustained that head injury, he might not know he has epilepsy?"

"Exactly. Even so, he had a VNS device implanted in his chest as a safeguard."

"I don't know what that is."

"It stands for vagus nerve stimulation. He wears a watch with a magnet in the underside of the strap. The magnet, when passed across Trey's chest, provides extra stimulation to the implant that might be necessary in situations likely to trigger a seizure, such as the flashing of multiple camera bulbs. Bottom line, the VNS implant is the equivalent of a pacemaker for epilepsy."

"Is the implant the reason Trey missed last week's race?"

Adam nodded. "It needed to be replaced. Trey probably could have been cleared to race this week, but his fiancée—who's also a doctor—insisted he sit out the upcoming race in Richmond."

"What happens if NASCAR finds out?"

"Nothing, because certain NASCAR officials know about Trey's condition. They've approved his racing. The problem is, I took the family's agreement to keep Trey's medical condition under wraps too far. I didn't tell Ethan or any of the team members. That turned out to have been a huge mistake."

Apparently, Hope surmised, this was the "rocky time" Ethan had alluded to when she'd asked him about his job.

"Keeping the truth about their driver from them, and then requiring them to sign a confidentiality agreement before they were told about Trey's condition, has eroded their confidence in me. I was hoping their trust would reestablish on its own over time. It hasn't."

"Counting on that is a common misconception when it comes to trust," Hope explained. "Helping you to regain your team's confidence is something we can certainly work on. But trust is complex and hard to earn. There's only one thing that builds it."

"What's that?"

"The way people behave. In this case, the way *you* behave from now on. You broke trust with your people. You have to rebuild it, sometimes over and over again."

"I'll do whatever it takes, for as long as it takes. Which is why you're here."

"Do you have the information that I asked you to compile?"

Adam nodded. "The packet's on my desk. It has a file on every member of the team, his or her job description and how long they've worked here."

"I'll study it tonight."

"Then what?"

"I'll develop a roadmap for you to use to rebuild and sustain trust with your employees."

"Sounds simple enough."

"It's anything but. To start, it's of vital importance that you announce to the team why I'm here. However, it would be counterproductive to tell them that *your* mistake has caused problems with *their* work. Instead, remind them that their teamwork has to be as finely tuned as the cars they work on. And you're wanting to find out if tweaking anyone's performance can get your cars to the checkered flag more often."

Adam nodded. "That's definitely the company's ultimate goal."

"I'll design a short survey for every employee to fill out. Then meet individually with each person. That'll help me understand which employees are having the toughest time. I'll also diagnose the entire team's strengths and weaknesses by observing their performance during normal workdays and also at various races. As I mentioned on the phone, I'm juggling work for other clients so I'm only able to spend a couple of days a week working for you."

"Not a problem. I've got Brent under contract to fly you between Charlotte and Dallas as often as necessary, and also to upcoming races. You just let my secretary know your schedule, and she'll coordinate things with Brent's office manager."

"Sounds good," Hope said. Then instantly realized that just the thought of climbing into the cockpit again and spending hours beside Brent Sanford—*smelling his compelling scent*—had her face heating.

She knew the heat must have settled as a blush in her cheeks when Adam frowned. "Was there a problem between you and Brent on the flight here?"

"No. I don't know anything about flying a plane, but your brother struck me as very efficient." She forced a smile. "He even taught me a little about navigating."

"Brent let you navigate?"

Hope raised a shoulder. "It helped pass the time." Especially after she'd tossed his past in his face, and silence had hung between them like a wet blanket. All because she'd panicked when the man put her hormones on point with one grin.

Damn her libido. And damn whatever it was about Brent Sanford that had jump-started it back to life after two years of blessed numbness.

Maintain a professional detachment, she reminded herself. That had always been her rule number one when it came to dealing with clients. Brent Sanford wasn't exactly a client, but his brother was. As far as Hope was concerned, that was good enough for her.

And so it should be. For heaven's sake, the man had gotten caught cheating. Just as blatantly as her fiancé had. She'd been deeply, desperately hurt by his actions. No way was she a glutton for punishment. She had learned her lesson.

So, whenever her path crossed again with Captain Sanford, she would keep things on a business basis.

No matter how good he smelled.

CHAPTER THREE

LATER THAT NIGHT, HOPE DROPPED onto one of the over-stuffed chairs in her father's den. "I don't know how you do it," she said while stifling a yawn. "I've only been here for one evening and I'm already toast."

Ensconced behind his massive desk, Dan Hunt peered around his computer monitor. "You don't know how I do what?"

"Keep up with Grace's kids." Having changed into gray drawstring pants and a tank top in eye-popping yellow, Hope propped her legs over one of the chair's arms and snuggled into its soft folds to get comfortable. "I spent an hour in the backyard playing ball with Matthew. Then after dinner, I got a lesson on what dolls are all the rage when Millie and Bella decided to put on a miniature fashion show in the upstairs hall. Sadie joined us when she and Ethan got here. I had to narrate while they toddled the dolls down their makeshift runway."

Chuckling, her father leaned back in his leather chair. His face was tan with crinkles at the edges of his eyes. He wore his thick, iron-gray hair closely brushed to his head. Now in his early sixties, the retired NASCAR crew chief was fit in a lean way that was genetics as much as hard work.

"Sorry, Hope, I can't give you much sympathy. Your mother ran herd on four kids full-time. And I couldn't lend her a lot of help because my job kept me so busy, not to mention gone a lot. You ask me, she's the one who had it rough."

"You're right," Hope agreed, her throat tightening at the mention of her mother.

Over the past months, the fierce pain of loss had turned into a dull ache. Still, there were times the void that Linda Hunt had left in her daughter's heart was almost unbearable. Hope imagined her grief was nothing compared to what her father felt at losing the wife he'd considered his soul mate.

While she waited for tears to stop stinging her eyes, Hope glanced around the warm, vibrant room where colorful rugs pooled on the hardwood floor and polished brasses shared space with books in the floor-to-ceiling shelves.

It was still so very easy to picture her mother dusting the books and knickknacks that filled those shelves. And visualize her parents on winter evenings, huddled in their respective leather chairs in front of the gray stone fireplace while flames danced and wood crackled.

Tonight, the fireplace's inner hearth sat empty and blackened by countless fires.

Hope's gaze narrowed on the dark abyss. She had loved her mother dearly, despite the heavy moods that seemed to plague her. Though Hope had suspected those moods were due to some secret past unhappiness, Linda Hunt had refused to talk about it on the few times Hope had brought up the subject. Not so long ago, Hope had come to the re-alization that it was her pressing need to help her mother that had steered her toward her work as a psychologist.

"And the good news is that neither of us had to cook tonight," Dan added.

"True," Hope said, shifting her gaze back to her father. She noted the faint layer of dust edging the untidy stacks of papers on his desk, something her mother never would have let happen. Hope made a mental note to give the house a thorough cleaning before she wound up her work for Sanford Racing and headed home to Dallas.

"When Grace picked up the kids tonight, she mentioned she has your freezer filled with casseroles," Hope added.

"Wonderful stuff," Dan replied, giving his flat belly a pat. "Plus, your big sister brings me a box of hors d'oeuvres on the nights she has catering jobs and I watch the kids for her. I consider that an even trade-off."

"I would, too." Just remembering the yummy-tasting pastry-wrapped pâté Grace had provided that evening started Hope's mouth watering. She decided to make a side trip to the kitchen for leftovers before she headed upstairs to tackle the employee files Adam Sanford had given her.

Speaking of work, she needed to get started.

Sighing, she swivelled her legs off of the chair's arm and rose. "I've got files I need to go over tonight, so I'd better get to them." She stepped around the desk, leaned in and pressed a kiss to the top of her father's head. Just catching a whiff of his familiar spicy aftershave he'd worn for as long as she could remember made her feel even more at home. She wondered if there was some small nook or cranny in the house that still harbored the soft, flowery scent her mother had always worn.

Hope swallowed around the lump in her throat. "I'm glad I'm here, Daddy."

He snagged her hand, squeezed it. "So am I." His forehead furrowed as he gazed up at her.

"What?" she asked.

"I don't like you living halfway across the country. I miss you."

"I miss you, too. But Dallas is where my job is."

"Seems to me your job has brought you home."

"For a time." Hope had attended a Texas university on a scholarship and after graduation she'd accepted a job with a Dallas-based company. Later, she'd opened her own business there to be in close proximity with her academic and business contacts. Not to mention the man she'd fallen in love with. All those considerations had made Big D the perfect base of operations for her. And for her oil man fiancé who'd turned out to have a secret penchant for conning wealthy widows with pots of old Texas money.

With that painful experience behind her, Hope had recently found herself toying with the idea of relocating her company to Charlotte. But she hadn't yet made a decision, and wasn't ready to talk to anyone about it, not even her father.

"I'll be popping in and out of your life for a while, so you might get tired of having me around," she said lightly. "I told Adam Sanford the only way I could do the consulting job for him now was to squeeze him in with other clients. He agreed, so I'll be doing a lot of flying around the country for the next few weeks."

"With Brent Sanford at the controls."

The ripe disgust in her father's eyes sounded in his voice. He'd been crew chief for the NASCAR Sprint Cup Series team whose car Brent had bribed a man to sabotage, and Dan Hunt had taken the entire incident personally.

Hope lifted a shoulder. "Brent is who Adam hired to fly me."

"Adam Sanford's a good man. His brother is a cheater."

"That doesn't make him a bad pilot," she retorted. It was Hope's turn to furrow her forehead. Why the heck did she feel the need to defend the man? After all, what her father said was nothing more than the truth.

"I'll concede that the man's a good pilot. That doesn't mean I have to like the idea of my baby daughter having contact with someone who'd step over the line to win a race."

"Even so, Brent is scheduled to fly me to several races, the first being in Richmond this weekend." She squeezed her father's shoulder while reminding herself her number one goal was to get her libido under control before she climbed into another plane with Brent. "So, just concentrate on the fact that the man at the controls is an ace pilot." Which was advice she planned to take herself.

"I'll give it my best shot." Dan's fingers tightened on hers. "Speaking of men, is there one in your life these days?"

"Hardly," Hope scoffed. "I swore off the male species, remember?"

"You swore off scoundrels like David Preftakes." Her father's eyes darkened. "He out of prison yet? If so, I'd like to invite the bastard to meet me in a dark alley so I can teach him a lesson for hurting my little girl."

"He's still locked up. And even if he was out, I wouldn't want you anywhere near him."

Dan shook his head, watching her. "He was good at fooling people, Hope. I understand that's made you gun-shy, but there's a lot of men out there who are honest and trustworthy."

She tweaked her father's ear. "I'm waiting until I find one who's as honest and trustworthy as you."

Just then, the computer beeped. Hope's gaze went to the monitor. Her eyes went wide. "Daddy, are you in a chat room?"

"That's right." His hand slid from hers. "What, you've never chatted online with a friend?"

"Of course I have. It's just that you…"

"I what?"

"You were never into computers."

"Not until after I lost your mother." He shrugged. "When Grace picks up the kids at night, this place gets quiet. Sometimes too quiet. So I come in here and chat for a while. Doesn't do anybody any harm."

Hope had experienced her own brand of loneliness after her engagement tanked. She'd used work to fill her time and keep her mind occupied. But her father had retired from NASCAR when her mother had gotten sick. Although Hope's brother Jared planned to hire their father after Jared increased his business as an engine builder, Dan Hunt didn't presently have a job to fall back on.

And his wife wasn't the only person her father had lost recently. His best friend had been murdered at the end of last year while attending the banquet in New York City.

"Daddy, have you heard anything new about Uncle Alan's murder?" Alan Cargill hadn't been officially related to the Hunts, but as Dan's best friend he'd been as close as blood kin.

"Not a thing since they arrested that guy in July." Dan

scrubbed a hand over his face. "Even though things don't add up the police say it was a mugging that went bad. Doesn't surprise me—Alan wouldn't have given up his money and property willingly. Especially those diamond-studded gold cufflinks. They were his prized possession."

"I wish he had given them up without a fight," Hope said softly. "He might still be alive."

"I've thought that same thing about a hundred times."

When the computer beeped again, Hope slid her arms around her father's neck and hugged the man she adored most in the world. "Have a good chat, Daddy. I love you."

"I love you, too, baby girl."

AFTER DAYS OF DR. HOPE HUNT clinging to his thoughts like a burr, Brent dreamed of her.

Of a gorgeous face with sculpted cheekbones defined by a curve of lightly tanned skin. Of thick, straight hair, the color of warm whiskey. Of smoky-gray eyes.

"I was at the Talladega track four years ago," she told him, her voice ripe with censure. *"I know what you did."*

"You know what I was accused of."

Brent reached for her, his hands clamping onto her arms. Her haunting, maddening scent invaded his lungs. *"It was a setup."*

The top of her head reached his chin. When she tilted her head back, her full, coral-glossed lips parted slightly. He felt the rush of his own blood.

She gazed up at him, cool eyes watchful. *"What's the point of lying in your own dream? A guilty conscience eats at you from the inside out. I'm a psychologist. You can tell me the truth."*

"Fine," he said, pulling her down with him to his bed. *"I want you."*

Brent abruptly woke to an empty bed, empty arms and furious frustration.

"Holy hell," he muttered, sitting up. Hope Hunt was a menace. He'd spent years reinventing himself, putting his life back in order. Years of hard work and grueling hours while telling himself he didn't care one iota what anyone thought about him since he knew the truth. His conscience was clear because he hadn't bribed anyone. Hadn't done a damn thing wrong.

Period.

The only reality in the painfully erotic dream was that he wanted her.

A woman he'd met once. Hell!

He scrubbed his hands over his face and glanced at the clock on the nightstand. Today was Thursday, the good doctor and a regular passenger—a fifteen-year-old kid whose divorced parents had him shuttled between their homes a couple of times a year—were scheduled to meet him at the airport at 6:00 a.m. Brent planned to drop Hope in Richmond, Virginia, so she could observe the practices and qualifying round for Saturday's NASCAR Sprint Cup Series race. After he let Hope off, he'd fly the kid to Philadelphia where his mother lived. Another fare would be waiting for him there for a flight to Chicago. On Saturday—race day—he would return to Richmond.

But he wasn't just flying back there to pick Hope up. For the first time in four years, he planned to step foot on a NASCAR-sanctioned race track. And, he was sure, come face-to-face with former friends and coworkers who considered him a cheating scumbag.

If it had been anyone but Adam who'd asked him to show up at the track, Brent would have said no. But with their younger brother, Trey. still off the race schedule due to his replacement VNS implant, Adam needed the input of a driver he trusted to critique Shelly Green's performance—in person, not on video. Green was good, and she had a sponsor's interest. She'd already proven herself driving for Sanford Racing in the NASCAR Nationwide Series, and Adam was on the verge of offering her a NASCAR Sprint Cup ride for next season. He was holding off on that, though, until he had a seasoned driver's impartial critique on her performance.

It meant something, Brent thought, that Adam valued his opinion. *Trusted him.* Trey was a different matter.

One he didn't want to think about right now. Not with his head still full of what he'd dreamed of doing to Hope Hunt. *With her.*

Dammit, the last thing he would admit to anyone was that all of his senses told him it would be easier for him to show up at the Richmond track with her there. *Because* she was there. Why, he had no clue. He just knew it.

And that was one more confusing, maddening thing he didn't want to think about.

AFTER LEAVING THE HOUSE, Brent headed to the gym. He did a hard workout, pumping free weights and doing cardio, reminding his body that it wasn't built to simply sit behind the controls of an airplane. Pleased that the sweat he'd worked up this time had nothing to do with sexual fantasies, he showered, shaved and walked into Sanford Aviation at half past five.

Maureen Queen peered up at him from behind her computer's monitor. "Morning, boss. There's been a change in plans for the flight to Richmond."

Inside his belly, something twisted. Disappointment, Brent realized, at the thought that Hope might have cancelled.

"What change, Mo?"

"You've got an additional passenger hitching a ride."

The knot in his gut relaxed as the scent of fresh coffee drew him to the coffeemaker on the credenza behind her desk. "Who's the extra fare?"

"A NASCAR driver. He said something about missing the flight yesterday on his team's plane." Paper rustled as Mo flipped pages on her ever-present notepad. "He was going to fly to Richmond commercial, but decided it was too much of a hassle."

Brent took his first sip of coffee, and grimaced. Mo always brewed the stuff strong enough to fuel the Lear. "This guy have a name?"

"Zack Matheson. He drives for—"

"Matheson Racing," Brent said.

Mo jabbed a pencil into her gray topknot, then leaned back in her chair. "I take it you know him."

"Yeah." He and Matheson had both quit NASCAR racing the same year. Only difference was, Matheson hadn't left with a sabotage accusation hanging over his head. He'd rejoined his family's team at the beginning of the current season and had won at Daytona. Since then, his driving had been iffy.

Apparently not expecting more of an answer, Mo moved on. "I called the FBO. They've got the Skylane fueled and ready to go."

"Good." Brent braved another sip of Mo's lethal

brew. "I'll phone the weather service then get started on the preflight check."

"Just to let you know, Dr. Hunt called to verify she'll be here on time," Mo added, then smiled. "She sure is a talker at this time of the morning. Sounds perky. Bet she's one of those people who jumps out of bed all chipper and ready to tackle the day."

Brent thought of his dream. He'd like to find out for himself just how Hope acted in the morning after a night in his bed.

"Let me know when my passengers arrive."

THE FIRST PERSON HOPE SPOTTED when she walked into the small general aviation terminal building was the blonde behind the customer service counter. Four days ago, it hadn't sat well when the woman leaned across the counter and pressed a kiss to Brent's cheek after he handed her a small wrapped package.

That image *still* didn't sit well, and Hope was beyond frustrated.

What was wrong with her? It was a well-documented fact that Brent Sanford wasn't above cheating to get what he wanted. That particular character trait also described her ex-fiancé to a *T*. She'd dumped the rat, so why the heck couldn't she rid her thoughts of the pilot with the dark blotch on his past whom she'd met only a few days ago?

"Help you?"

Readjusting the strap of her briefcase over her shoulder, Hope wheeled her small carry-on to the counter. "I have a flight booked this morning through Sanford Aviation."

"Oh, you're one of the people flyin' with Brent." The

woman's vivid blue eyes sparkled and Hope had to admit that her slight Southern drawl sounded captivating.

"That's right."

"Lucky you. The man is a doll."

Hope lifted a brow. "You think so?"

"I *know* so." Slim, with a peaches-and-cream complexion, the woman rested a well-toned forearm on the counter. "My son, Joey, collects miniature die-cast NASCAR race cars. He needed one more to have a complete set, but it was one of the first made. Rarer than cold weather in the tropics. My husband and I couldn't find it anywhere, not even on eBay! About a month ago, I mentioned to Brent that we were looking for the car for Joey. Last Monday was his birthday, and Brent showed up here with the car, all wrapped in gold paper and tied with a red bow."

The woman shook her head. "Brent's office manager told me he added an extra two hours to a flight to divert somewhere so he could pick up the car from the guy who was selling it. Doesn't that just beat all?"

"Yes, it does," Hope murmured. So much for her assumption that Brent had been delivering a gift to one of the numerous conquests he'd been rumored to have made during his days as a NASCAR driver.

"He's one of the most thoughtful people I know," the blonde gushed as she reached for the phone. "I'll just give Brent's office manager a call to tell her you're here."

Hope sensed another presence behind her just as a deep voice asked, "Are you talking about Brent Sanford?"

The receptionist shifted her gaze past Hope. "That's right. Are you flying with Sanford Aviation, too?"

"I am," the man said as he stepped beside Hope. He

was just under six feet tall with dark hair. Gray eyes nearly the same color as hers stared out from a tanned, handsome face. "I'm Zack Matheson."

"I'll let Mo know you're both here," the receptionist said as she stabbed buttons on her phone.

"Matheson," Hope said, regarding him. "As in Matheson Racing?"

He grinned. "As in. And you are?"

"Hope Hunt."

His eyes narrowed. "Hunt, as in Jared, Ethan and Grace?"

"As in," Hope said. "And Dan. He's my dad."

The receptionist ended her call. "Mo suggested y'all have a seat in the reception area. Brent'll be in to get you as soon as he completes his preflight check."

Zack grinned down at Hope. "If I had Sanford's cell number, I'd call and tell him to take his time." He swept an arm toward a small seating area near a collection of vending machines. "How about I buy you a cup of coffee, Hope Hunt?"

He was good-looking, with a come-and-get-me grin and friendly demeanor. Yet, she didn't feel the stirring pull deep down inside that she'd felt in Brent's presence. Not even a small tug.

What, she wondered, was wrong with her?

AFTER WRAPPING UP HIS preflight check, Brent strode into the private terminal's brightly lit lobby. As often was the case in the early morning hours, people milled around, waiting for their chartered flights. The warm, heavy scent of yeast and cinnamon drew his attention toward the far side of the building where a line had formed outside the café. The place was constantly busy, having earned nationwide recognition for what it billed as the "world's greatest cinnamon rolls."

Turning a corner, Brent aimed his gaze toward the seating area bordered by vending machines—and spotted Zack Matheson kneeling at Hope Hunt's feet.

Not kneeling, Brent amended as he got closer. Crouching was more like it, while he tugged something out of a duffel bag.

Brent recognized the "something" the instant Matheson stood and held it up for Hope's perusal. The electric-blue ladies' nightshirt came from Matheson's NASCAR merchandise line. The No. 548 emblazoned across the front was his driver number. The blue represented Matheson Racing's team color.

The NASCAR Sprint Cup Series driver's smile signified a male's unconcealed interest in a woman.

The smile was damn irritating.

At least to Brent. The doc, however, didn't seem to have a problem with it.

Her mouth curved as Matheson nudged the nightshirt into her hands. "I'll wear it tonight," she said.

"Knowing that, I doubt I'll get any sleep," he replied.

Aware that his jaw had locked tight, Brent stepped forward. "Morning," he managed.

Hope turned at the sound of his voice. She wasn't dressed in business mode today, he noted, taking in her dark slacks and cream-colored turtleneck, with a lightweight black leather jacket worn open. She'd swept her dark hair back in a sleek style that made him think of elegant parties under crystal chandeliers. Maybe she thought today's look was professional, but it was sexy enough to make his mouth water.

She sent him a cheery smile. "Good morning."

She sparkled, he thought. The sun wasn't even up yet, and the woman freaking sparkled.

While she slid the folded nightshirt into a zippered compartment on her small suitcase, Brent shifted his attention to Matheson. "It's been a while," he said, offering his hand.

"A long while." Matheson returned the handshake.

He'd rather be shaking Hope's hand, Brent thought. Did the woman have to smell so damn good everywhere she went?

"I've got one more passenger booked for this flight," he said. "His dad called the office to say their ETA is less than five minutes."

"His dad," Matheson repeated. "Do Hope and I have to babysit?"

"You be the judge," Brent said when he spotted the tall, gangly teenager coming their way. The kid was dressed in jeans and a red sweatshirt. Wires from earbuds hung down from both ears and he had a basketball tucked under one arm.

"Goodness," Hope said, following Brent's gaze. "He is one tall young man."

"Six-five at last count," Brent replied.

"Tell me he's an ace with that basketball," Zack Matheson said. "And that he's planning on going to college somewhere in the great state of North Carolina."

"Or Texas," Hope added, putting in a vote for her adopted state.

"Don't get your hopes up," Brent told her. "Todd'll play here, or in Pennsylvania where his mom lives. Which is where I'm flying him after I drop you two off in Richmond."

When Todd reached them, Brent made the introductions. And although his preference was to have Hope beside him during the flight, there was an issue of passenger comfort he needed to deal with.

"Todd, we'll put you in the copilot's seat where there's more leg room."

"Yeah, okay. That works," Todd said, then went back to listening to his music.

Matheson smiled down at Hope. "Looks like you and I get to share the backseat."

"Looks like," she said breezily.

His shoulders as rigid as steel, Brent grabbed the handle of her suitcase before Matheson had a chance to. He motioned for Todd to join them, then led the group out onto the tarmac.

The muscles in Brent's shoulders remained tight until they landed in Richmond a while later and Matheson drove off with the team member waiting to pick him up.

As far as Brent was concerned, it'd been hard enough having the first woman he wanted to be near in a long time sitting in the backseat of his Cessna. Harder, even, to listen to the breezy banter she and Matheson shared.

As he carried two cups of coffee toward the table Hope had commandeered in the terminal's small café, he wondered if Matheson had asked her out before leaving with the team member. The man was an idiot if he hadn't.

"I hope Todd doesn't think he's not welcome to join us," Hope said.

Brent glanced across his shoulder before settling in the chair beside hers. The kid had found a stool at the counter. Earbuds in place and basketball wedged under one foot, his thumbs raced across the keyboard of his cell phone. "He usually catches up on texting between flights."

Hope blew on her coffee before taking a sip. His gaze lingered on her mouth while he conjured up the memory of the way her coral-glossed lips had parted slightly in his dream. He felt the rush of his own blood, and this time he was wide-awake.

"That can't be easy for him," she began, "being ferried between divorced parents. Do you have a lot of clients who hire you to fly their kids to and fro?"

"A handful. Most of the kids seem to take it in stride." Brent checked his watch. All too soon his plane would be refueled and someone from Sanford Racing would arrive to pick Hope up. He didn't want to waste time talking about his job.

"How's your work for my brother going?" he asked.

"Slow and methodical, which is the norm for the beginning of a project. I've met individually with all of the employees. That's the first step when I do team building."

"How'd that go? Interacting with guys who know you've been hired to probe their minds?"

She sent him a pointed look. "Adam agreed to my request to explain to his people the first day why he hired me. I didn't want any of them to think I was there to play Ping-Pong with their brains."

"Draw any conclusions yet?"

"When I do, I'll discuss them with Adam."

Brent held up a hand. "He's your client, not me, I understand that. I just figure you'll be spending the next few days watching the team practice. Then observing them at the race on Saturday."

"That's right."

"If you want any pointers on race day, just ask."

Something flashed in her gray eyes. "You'll be there? At the track?"

"That's the plan." He lifted a brow. "Surprised?"

"Totally. Adam mentioned that you pretty much avoid anything NASCAR."

"He's right."

"So, why come to the race track this weekend?"

Because you'll be there. "Trey's still off the schedule. Adam needs an experienced, unbiased driver to evaluate Shelly Green's performance this weekend."

"Since he's letting her drive Trey's car, I would think Adam has a lot of faith in her."

"He does. But this isn't just about one race. He's considering offering her a NASCAR Sprint Cup ride next season. That's not something a team owner does lightly."

"Of course not." Hope's brow furrowed. "Have you been to many NASCAR races since…."

"Talladega," Brent finished when her voice trailed off. "Saturday will be the first time in four years that I've stepped foot on a NASCAR-sanctioned track. As you might imagine, I don't get the warmest welcome from most people in the business." It was his turn to give her a pointed look. "The majority of them think I'm a cheater who tried to sabotage a competitor's car."

Watching her gaze slide from his as she set her coffee aside told him she belonged in that category. "Some people don't share that opinion," she said.

"Really? Who?"

"The receptionist at the terminal in Charlotte. She told me about how you went out of your way to find her son a rare NASCAR miniature race car for his birthday."

"That wasn't a big deal."

"To her it was. She basically thinks you walk on water."

"Yeah?" Brent leaned in. "What do you think, Doc?"

"That someone who makes that kind of effort for a child must have some redeeming qualities."

"So, you think I maybe have some good points?"

"Everyone has good points. They're just sometimes hard to find."

"Want to try to find mine?"

She opened her mouth. He would never know what she had been about to say because at that moment, her name blared on the PA system.

"My ride's here," she said, then rose.

Brent stood, held out his hand. "See you at the track for the race, Doc."

She hesitated before she slid her palm against his. Her skin felt soft and warm, much the same as it had in his dream.

"See you," she replied, then grabbed the handle of her small suitcase and disappeared around a corner.

Too bad he couldn't get her out of his head that easily.

CHAPTER FOUR

"WANT TO TRY TO FIND MY good points?"

Brent's whiskey-soft words echoed in Hope's mind long after their chat at the Richmond airport.

His question niggled at her while she checked into the hotel room that Sanford Racing had booked for her. And during the following days while she drove to and from the race track. Even though she did her best to shove away the question—and all of its implications—over the long hours she spent observing the racing team's employees interacting on the job, it remained maddeningly at the periphery of her thoughts.

But it was at night when the memory of Brent's words hit her full blast, haunting her dreams.

Dreams that were so vivid and teeming with want that she woke up each morning antsy and unsettled.

She firmly believed, just as she'd assured Brent, that every person had their good points. Some more than others. But as far as she was concerned, a NASCAR driver who'd paid someone to sabotage the competition fell into the "others" category.

For the past two years she'd existed as the equivalent of a sovereign nation unto herself. By her own design, she lived alone and looked to no one else when it came time to make decisions. It wasn't as if she needed a man in her life in order to feel fulfilled. She was content, her business thriving, her friends numerous. Where men were concerned, she'd been chaste by choice. *Contentedly chaste.*

So why all of a sudden did she feel like the proverbial moth drawn to Brent Sanford's flame? It was a maddening question that she had no answer to. And had little time to try to come up with one.

After all, Adam Sanford had dug a deep hole for himself. It would take all of her skill and knowledge to help him climb out of it.

From her interviews with employees that included head mechanic, hauler driver, tire changer and part-time spotter she had confirmed her impression that keeping them in the dark about Trey Sanford's medical condition, then requiring them to sign a confidentiality agreement, eroded whatever trust they'd had in their boss. It didn't matter that Adam's motivation stemmed from a desire to keep media attention on Trey as the team's NASCAR Sprint Cup Series driver and off his health. Bottom line was, Adam's actions had made his workers feel as if the boss didn't trust them to keep Trey's condition to themselves. As a result, morale had declined, performance plummeted and employees became disengaged. A few had quit their jobs before Adam finally leveled with his people.

Hope knew that employees did not care about the needs of the business until it was clear that the business cared about *their* needs and well-being. Adam had a major task facing him. One she felt sure he could accomplish if he followed the operations plan she'd devised for him to rebuild and sustain trust.

Over the past days he'd gone out of his way to spend

an inordinate amount of his workday with employees, just listening to what they had to say. He'd shown up in the fabrication shop, the engine building area and the garage on a regular basis. Before leaving Charlotte, he'd even spent time visiting with the receptionist who also managed Sanford Racing's gift shop.

However, this evening Adam had little time for hanging with the worker bees. Or they with him.

Hope remembered from visiting various race tracks with her crew chief father, that on race days, some team owners spent the majority of their time schmoozing with the all-important bill paying sponsors. Said schmoozing was often done in one of the VIP suites that rose above certain sections of the grandstand seats.

She also recalled just how chaotic things became in the garages and the pits.

The Richmond track was no exception. If anything, the cool evening air that smelled of race fuel, exhaust and rubber seemed even more electrified since tonight's race was the final showdown before the last ten races that marked the Chase for the NASCAR Sprint Cup.

Substitute driver Shelly Green had qualified fourteenth for the race in the No. 483 car. Hope had her fingers crossed that the personable young woman would zoom over the finish line even higher up. Maybe even win. That alone would boost Sanford Racing team's morale.

Hope had chosen an out-of-the-way spot in the pits from where she could observe the employees at work. Considering the chill that had settled in the air, she was grateful for the garage's dress code that required shirts with sleeves and long pants. Her black turtleneck, gray slacks and lightweight leather jacket were just the ticket to keep the chill at bay.

With less than half an hour to go before the start of the race, noise emanated not just from the pits and garages, but also from the crowds in the grandstands that seemed skyscraper-tall.

The cacophony of noise had Hope feeling as if she were sitting in a huge lighted bowl with the thrum of revving engines, whir of air-ratchets, PA system announcements and conversations blasting around her.

Yet, all sound seemed to fade from her mind when she glanced across her shoulder and spotted Brent striding her way.

He looked lean, fit and ruggedly handsome in khaki pants and a lightweight sweater as dark brown as his eyes. Like her, he wore a lanyard around his neck that displayed credentials showing he was a part of the Sanford Racing team, which authorized his presence in the garage and pit area. His long legs carried him toward her, his gait brisk. The bright lights picked up highlights in his brown hair.

He looked, Hope thought as her stomach muscles tightened, outrageously sexy.

He's no better than the lying scum who broke your heart, she reminded herself.

Her gaze shifted to where Ethan stood, talking to two members of the pit crew. Part of Hope's team building expertise was the ability to match names to faces, so she easily identified the men with her brother.

Tall and burly with bulging biceps, Griff Fletcher was the crew's front tire changer. Beside him stood Luis Macha, the front tire carrier. During pit stops, it was Griff's job to leap off the infield's low concrete wall with an air-powered impact wrench, rush to the front right side of the car, drop to his knees, remove the lug nuts holding the tire to the car then jerk off the tire. At that instant, Luis would pass a new tire to Griff, helping him line up the glued-on lug nuts for tightening with the air wrench. Then they'd scurry to the car's left front side and repeat the action.

All totaling about fourteen seconds.

Like Ethan, the crew members were dressed in the team's blue and yellow colors. Headphones that would be used to communicate during the race rested on each man's shoulders.

Hope saw Luis's eyes narrow. Both he and Griff stared at Brent with cold expressions. When emotion flashed across Luis's face, Hope identified it as open hostility.

She closed her eyes while Brent's words echoed in her memory. *I don't get the warmest welcome from most people in the business.*

Still, despite that he'd brought his exile from all things NASCAR on himself, she couldn't help but feel a twinge of admiration that Brent had the fortitude to show up tonight. He could have easily turned down Adam's request and avoided what would no doubt be uncomfortable hours spent in the presence of countless people who considered him a lying cheat. Instead, he'd come as a favor to his brother.

So, Brent Sanford was the type of man who'd go out of his way to locate a rare miniature NASCAR race car for a little boy. And he was willing to put himself in an unpleasant situation in order to help his brother. In Hope's estimate, the man was racking up a lot of favorable points.

Which didn't exactly please her. His charmer's grin was already too appealing. He was too personable. Too sexy. Too…everything.

Seconds later, he reached the area where she sat near the pit box. On top were two crew members, busy checking the settings on several monitors located around the pit area that would show their driver's progress on the track. Both men glanced down at Brent, then looked away without acknowledging his presence.

Hope didn't miss the look of disdain the men exchanged between them.

The tick of a muscle in one side of Brent's jaw told her he'd noted the look, too. *Considering what you did, do you expect anything else?* she wondered.

"Doc," he said as he paused beside her chair. "How's business?"

"Keeping me off the streets and out of trouble." The warm scent of his woodsy cologne started a knot of nerves tingling at the base of her neck. Her shaky fingers toyed with the headset she'd yet to put on.

She sent Brent an easy smile that she hoped camouflaged her unsteadiness. "How's the air charter business, Captain Sanford?"

"I've racked up a lot of flight time since I dropped you off here."

"I take it you got Todd safely home to his mom in Pennsylvania?"

"Mission accomplished."

"Good to know." The monitor nearest her chair flicked to life, showing the starting line. "Did you hear that Shelly Green qualified fourteenth?"

"Adam called and updated me. He said she still doesn't like the feel of the car, and they're discussing adjustments. We'll see soon how everything comes together." Brent gestured in the direction of the infield. "I'm going to watch the race from on top of the hauler.

If Adam can get away from the team's sponsor, he'll meet me up there."

Hope nodded. The gigantic haulers were the equivalent of each team's mobile command center. In addition to providing a place for employees to relax and meet before and after the race, the garage-on-wheels housed the primary and backup cars, and enough parts and tools to repair an entire car. The viewing platform on top of the hauler made for a prime spot to watch the race.

But Hope wasn't there to watch the race. It was her job to observe the team at work during the race.

"I'll see you later," she said.

"If you run into Gaby Colson, ask her if she needs to ride with us to the hotel."

Hope hesitated. Although most Sanford Racing employees were scheduled to fly back to Charlotte tonight on the team plane, she had to return to Dallas for an important meeting with another client. Since there were storms all the way to Dallas, the plan was for her and Brent to wait until morning to take off from the general aviation airport where he'd tied down his plane.

Just the thought of them both spending the night in their newly reserved rooms at a nearby airport hotel had her on edge. But she knew she would be far more jittery if not for the fact that Gaby Colson, Trey Sanford's PR rep, would be sharing the room with her. And joining them on tomorrow's flight to Dallas.

"Actually, I'm riding to the hotel with Gaby." Hope had made a point to prearrange her transportation with the PR rep. The less time spent with the tempting Captain Handsome, the better. "My suitcase is already in her rental car."

"I see," Brent said. He loomed over her, tall and un-fathomable, staring down at her with dark eyes filled with so much awareness that she had to fight the urge to squirm in her chair.

Her reaction had her gritting her teeth. So what if he knew she wanted to avoid him? That was her right, wasn't it? Even so, it didn't stop her from feeling a twinge of guilt.

"I'll catch up with you at the hotel in the morning, then." His mouth hitched on one side. "Sleep tight, Doc."

"I'll do my best." *If* I can get you out of my head.

The sudden boom of pistons roaring to life filled the air. Instantly, Hope slid on her headset, then winced when her hair snagged on one of the earpieces.

"Hold on," Brent said.

In view of the noise, she read his lips more than heard the words. He slid a finger around the earpiece and freed the wayward strand. As he pulled his hand back, his fingertips grazed her cheek.

She felt his touch like a great gnawing ache, and was helpless to pull her eyes away from his. Not while heat coiled in her belly and a blush warmed her cheeks.

Lord, she didn't want to feel that heat. Or be aware of her heartbeat picking up speed and losing its steady rhythm. But it was difficult to control either reaction when a man like Brent Sanford stood looking at her as if he'd like to start nibbling at any single part of her body and keep going until he'd devoured it all.

And, try as she might, she couldn't deny there was a part of her that wanted him to.

Only when he turned and headed out of sight did she ease out a breath. Which was when she noticed Ethan frowning at her. The heat that already flamed in her face intensified.

Growing up, she'd seen Ethan's protective big brother look whenever certain males got overly friendly with his baby sister. And he'd been far from happy that he hadn't seen through her sleazy ex's false facade. Which had made Ethan even more protective of her. Still, she couldn't help but wonder if his frown was due more to Brent's reputation or from her obvious reaction to the man.

Just then, the announcer asked everyone to stand for the prayer. The first strains of the National Anthem sounded. Drivers climbed into their cars, then came the call, "Gentlemen, start your engines."

The cars filed out from pit road behind the pace car and began to lap the track, getting into their starting order as they moved.

Hope was still on her feet when the nearby monitor showed the green flag signal the beginning of the race. Cars shot across the start/finish line. Their combined engines sounded like mayhem. Or madness. Or the roar of a dozen huge planes.

While the swarm of cars raced toward Turn One, Ethan's voice sounded over her headset. "How's she feel, driver?"

"All good," Shelly Green replied.

Hope had done her research and knew that Richmond was one of the shorter tracks NASCAR utilized. The cars that stayed in the race until the end would do a total of four hundred laps. Hope settled in her chair for the duration.

The monitor showed Shelly heading round Turn One, her car's nose barely ahead of the No. 548 electric-blue car driven by Zack Matheson. He tried to hold

Shelly off, but failed. Shelly was too fast for Matheson, especially when they exited Turn Two.

"So far, so good," Ethan radioed.

On the monitor the cars entered Turn Three. By the time they approached the fourth turn, Shelly was a full car length ahead of Matheson.

Hope eased out a breath. Lap one down, three hundred ninety-nine to go.

Thirty laps later, Shelly was in tenth place. Hope knew it would soon be time for the car to pit. For years she'd heard her father talk about pit strategy, one of the most important parts of a race. As were yellow caution flags which could require the cars to slow down numerous times. When that happened, the amount of fuel used over a certain period changed, affecting a team's pit strategy in an instant.

Behind the wall, the Sanford pit crew waited for their driver's car to come in. They'd donned their required helmets and blue-and-yellow uniforms that made them look as if they belonged on the space station. Some gripped air-wrenches. Others balanced gas cans that looked like cruise missiles with elephant trunks. Another clenched a hydraulic jack. Although their expressions looked calm, Hope imagined the anticipation of giving their driver the fastest pit stop possible had their collective nerves coiled like a rattlesnake ready to strike.

The roar of the cars grew louder. Hope's heart began to pound. So much depended on a good, clean pit stop. One misstep could cost precious position out on the track. If the crew messed up, Shelly Green would wind up behind some of the cars she'd managed to pass.

Hope's shoulders tensed when Shelly steered off the track. A stream of cars followed behind her.

A sign man waved a long pole with a flag on its end so Shelly could spot the right pit area.

When her car was a few pit stalls away, Ethan's voice sounded over the headset. "Five, four, three," he said, to let his driver know how close she was to her team.

Even before the car fully braked, part of the crew was over the wall, the jackman stopping by the passenger-side door while the car came to a halt. Wrenches whirred. Motors revved. The crowd screamed. After about six seconds, the crew changed sides, repeated their synchronized maneuvers. With four new tires and a topped-off gas tank, the car roared away.

Halfway through the race Hope began to realize that Shelly might actually have a chance at winning.

After three-quarters of the laps were run, a car drove into Turn Three too hard and sideswiped the wall. Watching the monitor, Hope held her breath as another car grazed the first. Then another. One car spun out, crashed against the wall. All of it happened behind Shelly. *Thank goodness*, Hope thought.

The next time Shelly came into the pits, Hope's nerves were wound so tight that she sprang out of her chair as the crew went over the wall. At first, their move-ments seemed as finely tuned as the car they serviced. Then something slowed Griff Fletcher and Luis Macha's usual speed while changing the second front tire. Shelly's car roared away two, maybe three, seconds later than it should have—an eon in race car time.

Hope stepped back to the monitor. Shelly had come into the pit sixth, and came out tenth.

"What happened? What the heck happened?" Shelly's strained voice blasted through the headphones.

"Problem getting the second wheel lined up with the

axle," Ethan responded, his voice as hard as the pit's floor.

"Gotta make up the time," Shelly said.

"People, we need to do better," Ethan barked. "A lot better."

Hope knew that getting on to the crew was Ethan's job, but she still felt bad for the tire guys. Their mistake had cost Shelly precious seconds that she might not be able to make up.

She did a mental scroll through Luis Macha's personnel file. He'd only worked for Sanford Racing a few months, so he wouldn't have been affected by Trey's medical condition having been kept secret from him. *Mistakes happen*, she reminded herself.

Her gaze swept the pit area until she zeroed in on Luis. He'd flopped down on a stack of tires, his elbows on his knees, his head bowed. Clearly he knew he had screwed up.

Hope fought her ingrained team-building instinct to go talk to Luis. He wouldn't be receptive to hearing positive advice right now while he felt so dejected. And there wouldn't be time after the race to meet with him, either, since the team would immediately start packing and moving equipment and cars back into the hauler. So she made a mental note to talk to Adam and Ethan, give them both pointers on how to deal with Luis's blunder so it wouldn't put an already shaky team on even more unfirm ground.

When Hope turned her attention back to the monitor, she saw that there were ten laps to go. Shelly's car was in eleventh position. Hope's foot tapped against the war wagon's floor with sheer nervous energy.

Later, when the flagman waved the checkers on the final lap, Shelly's car still held that position.

Maybe because of one misstep during a pit stop.

Maybe not.

Her thoughts on the race, Hope removed her headset and made her way out of the pit. She passed through the restricted area, then stepped into a swarm of humanity that immediately enveloped her. Race track employees mixed with spectators and members of the media. As she wove her way through the crowd, the strain of the long hours she'd spent at the track over the past days caught up with her. Thankfully, the hotel near the small airport was just a short distance away. It would be a relief to climb into bed. And tonight, she promised herself, she wouldn't allow her thoughts to linger on Brent Sanford.

"Hope!"

Gaby Colson stood in the spot where they'd agreed to meet, the overhead lights making her reddish-gold curls shine.

Hope managed a tired smile. "I don't know about you, but I'm ready to get to our hotel."

"Change in plans," Gaby said, sending a rueful look Hope's way. "The PR gig I had in Dallas got postponed. Adam's approved my hitching a ride back to Charlotte on the team plane tonight."

Hope blinked. "You're not going to the hotel?"

"Nope. But don't worry about your suitcase. When I called Adam, he was on top of the hauler, watching the race with his brother. Brent said he'd drive you to the hotel, so Adam had one of his guys move your suitcase from my rental car to Brent's. He said to tell you he'd meet you here after the race."

Gaby glanced past Hope's shoulder. "There's Brent now."

Turning, Hope watched him stride their way. He had the sleeves of his sweater shoved up on his forearms and a hard look had settled in his eyes. Silently, she cursed the fact that her heartbeat picked up speed the closer he got.

He paused, nodded to Gaby then met Hope's gaze. "I hear you're stuck riding with me to the hotel." His tone was unemotional, his eyes brooding.

"Stuck, no," she replied, keeping her voice light. "And I appreciate your giving me a ride."

Gaby's cell phone chimed. She pulled it off the waistband of her slacks, checked the display. "I've got to take this," she said, sending them an apologetic look. "See you guys some other time." She answered her call and disappeared into the milling crowd.

Hope's instincts told her Brent had experienced a rough time tonight being surrounded by people who knew about the black smear on his past. Without conscious thought, she reached out, placed a hand on his bare forearm. And felt the heat of his flesh against her palm.

"I guess being here tonight wasn't easy for you."

"I didn't expect it to be." He shifted a step sideways, forcing her to drop her hand. "You ready to get out of here?"

"More than ready." As if trying to hold in the heat of his flesh, she curled her palm against her thigh. And damned the wave of empathy she felt for a man who was facing the consequences of his own dishonesty.

CHAPTER FIVE

DAMN, DAMN, DAMN!

He'd expected to get looks of disdain, Brent thought. Had known when he agreed to Adam's request to attend tonight's race that unless something phenomenal occurred on the Richmond race track, the presence of a disgraced former NASCAR driver would hardly go down like a shot of smooth whiskey.

He'd assured himself he was prepared for that. Had acknowledged that even though four years had passed, some people would never forget. Or forgive. Not when it came to cheating in a sport some considered almost holy. He was and—unless he found a way to clear his name—would forever be persona non grata when it came to anything NASCAR.

But, he realized as he nursed his second drink in the hotel's snazzy little bar, he hadn't factored Hope Hunt's presence at the race track into the muddy mix.

A huge error on his part.

It had been bad enough that he'd had to turn his back on a reporter who'd stuck a microphone in his face while demanding to know how it felt to be a disgraced driver returning to a rack track. Then he'd had to endure looks of contempt from people whom he had once considered colleagues. Friends, even. Worse yet that he'd discovered just how much more unsettling all that had been because Hope had witnessed some of it.

Which made no sense, considering he barely knew the woman.

What the hell kind of hold did she have on him, anyway? He could count on the fingers of one hand the times she'd actually been in his presence. Of course, if he factored in the sweaty dreams that had taken over his nights, he and the sexy Ph.D. were a hell of a lot more than casual acquaintances.

"Get you another one of those?"

The question had Brent looking across the polished wood bar with a sparkling mirror behind it. The bartender was a six-foot redhead with a beauty mark on the left side of her mouth. She looked as classy as the cozy room that boasted silver-topped tables, a handful of them occupied with couples murmuring in low tones. The warm yellow walls displayed photographs of plantations in and around the city that had once been considered the capital of the Confederacy.

He checked his watch, considering things. He could go up to his room, turn on the TV and try to lose himself in some show. But for reasons he couldn't explain, solitude didn't appeal to him tonight. Which was why he'd ventured downstairs after checking in.

"Sure." He lifted a brow. "Make it a double this time."

The redhead grinned. "Coming up."

His gaze tracked her as she hip-swayed away. In his carousing days, he would have already known her name and smooth-talked her phone number out of her. But the days when he'd built his life around speed—fast cars and even faster women—were long gone. He'd have been a fool to continue down that road when he had reason to believe the way he'd dealt with some woman in his past was why he'd been set up by Mike Jones.

Mike Jones, who had disappeared like smoke in the wind.

Brent tossed back the remainder of his drink, then leaned back on the padded bar stool to wait for the next. Because of the scandal and the amount of energy it had taken to get his aviation business off the ground—literally!—he'd managed to keep his mind off women. Mostly. Until Hope Hunt sauntered across the tarmac in her sexy black business suit, showing a mile of finely shaped leg.

Somehow, someway, she had pushed him over the edge of restraint he'd carefully maintained, from caution to out-and-out, no-holds-barred, can't-deny-it lust.

Yet, the way he'd dealt with her tonight when he'd caught up with her after the race proved just how rusty he was, woman-wise. It hadn't helped that she'd earlier made no effort to hide the fact that she'd arranged for a ride to the hotel with Gaby Colson in order to avoid him.

He suspected Hope had sensed his brooding mood because Miss Sunny Disposition barely said a word during the drive. Spoke little while they'd checked in. Murmured only a quiet, "Good night," when she stepped off the elevator to go to her room, located at the opposite end of the hall from his.

His mood had been so dark that for the first time since he'd met her, his mind didn't even wander to what moves he might have made if he didn't have the rep of being a cheater. Why bother thinking about those types of moves when the first woman he'd wanted in years had good reason to avoid him?

He was mildly surprised to find that his situation somehow seemed just as dire now as it had right after the scandal broke at Talladega. It was as if no time had passed to dull the shock of having the life he had planned out, plotted meticulously, and implemented with deliberation and simple hard work shatter.

To this day, he still didn't know why. Nor did he have any idea what had prompted the owner of Cargill Motors to mention to Adam Sanford at the NASCAR awards banquet that he'd learned something that made him question Brent's guilt in the sabotage. But Alan Cargill had been murdered before he had a chance to reveal what that something was.

It was all enough to drive a man to drink.

"Captain Sanford, do you have the time?"

Hope's voice jerked him back to the present as he met her gaze in the mirror over the bar. She stood a few feet from his stool, one forearm cocked so she could see her watch while a small plastic bag dangled from her fingers. He swivelled his stool, took her in.

She'd changed into black cropped pants and a loose white shirt that made him think of lazy Sunday mornings spent sprawled on the couch with the Sunday paper. Or maybe in bed. Her gleaming dark hair was pulled straight back from her flawless face and anchored behind her ears with a tortoiseshell headband. Diamond studs glittered at her earlobes.

The scent of her—creamy soap and skin—stirred every hunger he'd ever known.

"This a trick question, Doc?" he asked, nodding toward her watch. "Looks to me like you already know the time."

"I do," she said coolly. "I was just wondering if you're aware of it."

"How about we cut to the chase and you tell me why you're asking?"

"All right." She sent a pointed look at his glass that held only a few melting cubes of ice and a lime wedge. "You were supposed to fly me to Dallas in the morning."

"As far as I know, those plans haven't changed."

"They're changed because you're sitting in a bar, *drinking*. Correct me if I'm wrong, but doesn't the Federal Aviation Administration have restrictions on pilots consuming alcohol a certain number of hours before a flight?"

"It does."

She gave a curt nod. "I have to say I'm not one bit surprised to find you here."

"No? Why's that?"

"You're known to be a fan of sidestepping rules. Or trying to, anyway. This appears to be just another attempt."

The accusation in her voice had his eyes narrowing against a swell of anger. He'd had his fill of contemptuous looks and snide comments for one evening. "I suppose you could assume that about me, considering my past."

"I'm not *assuming* anything. Seeing is believing."

"Here you go," the bartender said as she settled his drink on the napkin she'd placed on the bar. "Straight tonic water with a wedge of lime, double on the lime." She shifted her attention to Hope. "What can I get for you?"

Even in the room's dim light, he saw the rush of color that stained Hope's cheeks.

"You're drinking tonic water? No vodka? No gin?"

"That's right. But maybe you ought to taste it for

yourself." He flicked a hand toward the glass. "That way, you won't have to depend on my word, which is apparently suspect, me being one of those people who likes to sidestep the rules and all."

He watched her shoulders square beneath the white shirt. Lifting her chin, she turned toward the bartender. "Do you have crow on the menu?"

The redhead's gaze flicked from Hope to Brent, then back to Hope. Her mouth twitched. "Sorry, I served the last plate of crow an hour ago. How about a glass of wine instead?"

"Make it Scotch, straight up."

"You got it." The woman placed a napkin on the counter beside Brent's drink before moving off.

He waited while the silence stretched out, ten seconds, then twenty, before Hope remet his gaze. "I'm once again in the position of owing you an apology."

Snagging his glass off the bar, he settled back on his cushy stool and studied her. The usual cheeriness in her gray eyes had been replaced by strain, and her fingers had a death grip on the plastic bag. If she hadn't looked so miserable he might have made a point to hold on to his anger. Or at least indulged in some serious gloating.

"You're not exactly the first person to think the worst about me."

"I'm sorry, Brent. I don't usually jump to conclusions." She rubbed two fingertips across her forehead, as though an ache had settled there. "My only excuse is that my schedule tomorrow is tight. When I passed by here on my way from the gift shop and saw you, all I could think was that you wouldn't be able to fly me to Dallas in time to make my first appointment." She lowered her hand. "That's no excuse for my tossing out accusations instead of being up-front and just asking what you're drinking."

Gazing at her, he wondered if he was a glutton for punishment by not just turning away from someone who made no secret she disapproved of him. Deciding to think about that later, he used one foot to pull out the stool beside his. "Take a load off."

When she slicked her tongue over her top lip, need crawled into his stomach and began to twist slowly. *That,* he knew, was a big part of the reason he couldn't bring himself to totally avoid her.

She glanced at the stool, then hesitated. "Are you sure you want my company?"

"You'll be the first to know if I don't."

"Fair enough."

She slid onto the stool, the movement having an interesting effect on her shapely curves beneath that tidy white blouse. His fingers tightened on his glass. He could feel himself falling into something with her that he wasn't sure he could handle, didn't especially want. But hell if he could resist her.

He watched her place the plastic sack bearing the hotel gift shop's logo on the bar. "What's in the bag?"

"I picked up a couple of granola and fruit bars for tomorrow." Her mouth curved. "The airline I fly serves only peanuts."

"That so? You could always go commercial."

"And miss out on my flight navigation lessons? I don't think so. Besides, word is, the guy who's been flying me around is one of the best pilots in the business."

"Anyone ever tell you that word of mouth isn't always accurate?"

"I may have heard that somewhere." She paused

while the bartender delivered her drink. After the redhead moved away to wait on the middle-aged couple who'd settled at the end of the bar, Hope added, "But in this case, I'm not relying on hearsay. I've actually flown with the guy and lived to tell about it. Twice."

"Lucky you."

"I think it's due more to your skill than my luck." She sipped her Scotch, regarding him over the rim of her glass. "Speaking of skill, what did you think about Shelly Green's driving tonight?"

"She's got potential."

"Enough for Adam to move her next season from the NASCAR Nationwide Series to the Sprint Cup?"

"Looks like." He tipped back his drink. "Certain tactics are used in the NASCAR Nationwide races that aren't smart to use in the NASCAR Sprint Cup. Shelly proved tonight she's aware of that."

"What sort of tactics?"

"The bump and draft for one. If you get your car right up behind another one, the two of you share a single tunnel of air."

"I remember hearing my dad talk about drafting. He said the tail end of the lead car becomes loose and light. All it takes is a bump to make it unstable."

"That's right. Shelly used a different tactic tonight. A smart one. If that pit stop hadn't slowed her down, she might have finished better than she did."

He watched Hope's brow furrow. "What?" he asked.

"The pit stop. Things had gone so smoothly with the pit crew when I watched them during weekly practices. Their movements were seamless. Synchronized. But tonight, something happened."

"Mistakes happen. You've got seven crew members

who have a specific job to do once they jump over the wall. You can't expect a perfect performance every time."

"I suppose not."

"You don't sound convinced. Don't you believe in human error?"

"Of course. I also believe that things are rarely as simple as they look."

"Not a surprise to hear, since you play Ping-Pong with people's brain cells for a living."

He watched the light bloom in her eyes, wishing he could touch her. Just once. Just for a moment.

"I would be more than happy to play Ping-Pong with your brain cells, Captain Sanford."

"I already told you that I don't need fixing."

"So, you did. Still, the mind is full of unanswered questions. Wouldn't you like to find the answers to some of yours?"

"I've already got all the answers I need." Most, anyway. He still didn't know why Mike Jones set him up.

"If so, you're a very fortunate person."

He watched her take another sip of Scotch. It hit him then that her eyes seemed more silver than gray tonight, and he wondered at their change. Seems as though he had some unanswered questions about her. No time like the present to try to remedy that.

"So, Doc, this is a Saturday night. If you were home in Big D, what would you be doing?"

"I'm not sure." She shrugged. "Laundry, maybe."

"Doing laundry on a Saturday night doesn't sound too exciting. Of course, that depends on whose laundry is mixed in with yours."

Her forehead furrowed. "Is this your way of finding out if I'm seeing someone?"

"I'm doing my best to be subtle. My technique might need work."

"Lots."

To GIVE HERSELF A MOMENT to think, Hope sipped her Scotch. Just the thought of his wanting to know if she was seeing someone had started her body humming. Which was a very bad thing. Brent Sanford was not the type of man she would ever again get tangled up with. There was no future in getting to know him better. If she danced around the truth and told him she was seeing someone, that would effectively slam the door on the possibility of any involvement.

Problem was, despite her best intentions, she found she didn't want to slam that door. Not even shut it all the way.

A little bubble of panic rose in her throat, and she slanted him a look. In the bar's dim light, the prominent planes of his face looked glass sharp. It was the kind of face that haunted a woman's secret dreams. Which was something she knew for a fact.

She felt the knots in her shoulders tighten. What the heck was she doing, sitting in a bar beside him? He was the last man she should be spending time with, but here she was.

And here was where she wanted to be.

"These days, the only laundry I do is my own," she said. All she could think was his nearness must be short-circuiting her brain cells.

"These days," he repeated. "Hasn't always been that way?"

"I was engaged once. Things didn't work out."

"Bad luck for him."

"Why, Captain Sanford, I think you just paid me a compliment."

One corner of his mouth quirked. "My way of being unsubtle."

Lord, why did she have to find the man so likable? *So appealing.*

A slight movement caught Hope's eye. Glancing over Brent's shoulder, she spied the middle-aged woman with a blond beehive sitting at the end of the bar. She kept her gaze locked on Brent while she leaned in to whisper something to the man beside her. He rolled his eyes as his companion slid off her stool and moved their way. Hope watched the look on her face grow more expectant the closer she got.

"Oh, I can't believe it," the woman exclaimed. "Oh, my God. Wendell, I was right. It *is* Brent Sanford!"

Although they weren't touching, Hope could have sworn she felt Brent flinch.

"Mr. Sanford, my husband and I are huge NASCAR fans," the woman said. "We never miss a race. You used to be my favorite driver until that…well, *unfortunate* incident at Talladega."

"Always nice to know I was somebody's favorite," Brent said.

Hope glanced over at Wendell. He was plump with a gingery mustache and a thin section of lank hair brushed across a balding skull. Since he was doing another eye-roll, Hope figured he was used to his wife's behavior.

"Your brother Trey does a good enough job on the track," the woman added. "But he just isn't you."

"That so?" Brent asked, giving her a deadpan look. "You think I drove better than Trey does?"

"Honey, there's no comparison."

Hope lifted a brow when Brent's expression turned smug. "I'll be sure and tell him."

"Now, don't you dare go and hurt your baby brother's feelings," the woman ordered as she shoved a small pad of paper and a pen into Brent's hands. "How about an autograph?"

"You really want an autograph from someone who hasn't raced for four years?"

"Of course." She flapped one hand in the direction of the pad. "If you could just sign 'To Wendell and Neva.'"

He scrawled on the pad, handed it back to her.

"This is wonderful," she gushed. "We're from Oklahoma City, and just love everything NASCAR. I know every little bit of trivia there is to know about the sport. I could talk racing all night long."

Sensing the woman was about to do just that, Hope touched her arm. "I'm sorry to interrupt, but we have an early flight in the morning. We were just about to leave when you stopped by."

"Oh, no problem." Neva glanced down at the pad, her smile beaming. "I can't wait to tell all our friends I got the autograph of one of the bad boys of racing."

"Do you get that often?" Hope asked a few minutes later as she and Brent stepped off the hotel's elevator. The corridor was long, dimly lit and deserted.

"Get what? Requests for autographs? Or referred to as a bad boy of racing?"

"Either." She turned to face him. Since their rooms were at opposite ends of the hallway, this is where they would part. "Both."

"I haven't had anybody ask for my autograph in a couple of years. As for the 'bad boy of racing' moniker, that got used a lot by the media right after Talladega. In most cases, it was a headline plastered over my picture."

"What happened then follows you around, doesn't it?"

Gazing down at her, he nodded slowly. "You have no idea how much."

"What about your brother Trey?"

"What about him?"

"You're not going to tell him what Neva said, are you?"

"About me being the better driver?" Brent shrugged. "Depends."

"On what?"

"Some things between Trey and myself that go back a few years. Not worth mentioning."

"You might want to consider that Trey goes back to driving for Sanford Racing next week in New Hampshire. Your telling him you met a fan who doesn't think his driving's topnotch might be detrimental not just to Trey, but the entire team."

"Which could put a speed bump on your road to getting Adam's employees back in shape."

"Could."

"I'll take that under advisement."

"Good." She held out her hand for the gift shop sack he'd picked up off the bar. "I'll say good night here. See you in the morning."

"Hold that thought until we get to your door," he said as he gripped her elbow and nudged her toward her room.

"You don't have to walk me," she managed, which wasn't easy, considering the touch of his fingertips against her skin had nearly frozen her lungs.

He flashed her a grin. "Didn't I mention that Sanford Aviation provides security service for all of its navigators?"

She couldn't help but smile. Dámmit, why did the man have to be so irresistible? "I guess informing me about that little perk must have slipped your mind," she commented with a forced casualness.

"Guess so."

When they reached the door to her room, she drew her elbow from his grasp and pulled her key card out of the pocket of her capris. She wanted, needed, to put some distance between herself and this man who evoked such disturbing responses within her.

"Too bad our conversation got interrupted in the bar," he commented.

She looked up at him. "Did it?"

He offered her the sack. "You were in the process of telling me about how your engagement didn't work out."

"Actually, that's all I intended to say." When she reached for the bag, he didn't release it, just tangled his fingers with hers. "It's not … a subject I like to talk about."

"Understood." He stepped closer. "So, you're not involved with anyone." He used his free hand to curl a strand of her hair around his fingertip. "Neither am I."

She didn't move. She couldn't. He had stepped so close she could feel the warmth of his breath on her cheek, could see the glint of passion in those dark eyes. Dark eyes that stared into her own, willing her to be still, to not pull away.

"Sounds like a coincidence," she breathed.

He dipped his head lower. "A convenient one that we maybe should take advantage of."

No. She wasn't sure if she spoke the word or merely thought it. Either way, it didn't matter. What had been building between them practically from the first moment they'd met was too strong to be denied by a feeble protest.

Her thoughts scattered as his thumb ran across her lips, pulling gently at them so that they opened slightly. Her breath shuddered out.

"How could any man who's ever kissed these lips possibly let you go?"

She could barely breathe now. Her body felt rigid as she fought with all of her self-control to rein in her emotions.

His hands moved to her shoulders. Through her white shirt she could feel the strength in them. The power. He pulled her close.

"Hope," he whispered, his voice a soft endearment.

Her lips parted slightly to murmur a protest. But before she could speak, his mouth was on hers, tender yet persistent. Her lips parted even farther, and the sensation of warmth turned into a raging fire.

Without thinking, her free hand went to his chest. But instead of pushing him away, her fingers curled into his sweater.

He murmured her name again as his lips left hers and moved to brush lightly across her cheek, her jaw, down the line of her throat. Then they returned to her mouth with a groan of desire that sent shivers up her spine.

Her lips parted on a quiet moan. He slipped his tongue between them, taking his time, and when she began to tremble, he shifted angles and lazily took the kiss deeper.

Her blood pulsed. She was drowning, sliding down where the air was too thick to breathe.

Her mind clouded, and her body took over, a sweet and steady ache.

"Let me come into your room." His voice was rough and husky and sounded something akin to a plea. "Let me have you tonight, Hope."

She wanted to. Heaven knew she wanted to! It would be so easy to unlock the door to her room, tug him inside. Take and be taken.

Just then, the elevator doors halfway down the hallway slid open with a soft whoosh that seemed to echo in Hope's ears. She heard laughter; her eyes flew open as two couples stepped into view and headed their way.

It was as if their presence dumped a cold bucket of sanity on her head. She pulled back abruptly. "This isn't what I want."

Brent kept his head dipped toward hers. A trick of the light made his eyes gleam with their own illumination. "That's not the signal you were sending," he said quietly.

"I know." She squeezed her eyes shut. "I know." She'd clenched her fingers around the gift shop bag so tightly that the granola bars inside felt like mush.

Much like her brain at the moment. Holy heaven, her legs were shaking, along with her hands. What the heck was the matter with her? She needed to draw her defenses together and nip this in the bud here and now. Otherwise, she might not survive intact.

She drew in a deep breath, and waited until the two couples disappeared into separate rooms.

"You remember my mentioning I had an ex-fiancé?" she asked, not surprised to find her voice shaky with emotion.

"Yeah, the guy with the bad luck."

"I made a mistake getting involved with him. A *big* one. That situation made me cautious about certain… issues." Like men who weren't above cheating others in order to get what they wanted.

"Want to share those issues with me?"

"No." She slicked her tongue over her bottom lip, and tasted him all over again. The trembling in her knees intensified. Allowing herself to respond to him, *to kiss him back*, was crazy. She couldn't afford even a short side trip into insanity.

"Suffice it to say it would be wise not to repeat what we just did."

"Do you always do what's wise?"

"I try."

He straightened, took a step back. "I don't like your decision, Doc. But it's yours to make, so I'll respect that."

"Thank you. Good night."

Her hands were shaking so badly, it took her two tries to slide the key card into the lock. When she stepped into the room, she closed the door and propped her back against it. Closed her eyes.

She wondered if he was still standing on the other side. Wondered if the kiss had affected him as fiercely as it had her.

"He's the last man on earth you should be kissing," she whispered.

Trouble was, he was the only man she wanted to kiss.

CHAPTER SIX

THE FOLLOWING MORNING'S FLIGHT from Richmond to Dallas had been filled with huge blocks of silence. For once in his career as an aviator, Brent welcomed the turbulent weather that kept his mind focused on flying and off of the woman sitting in the copilot's seat.

Mostly off of her, anyway. He couldn't completely rid his thoughts of the kiss they'd shared that had left him struggling to cling to the fine edge of reason.

For most of the flight, Hope kept her attention on the map and her navigating duties, so he had no idea what she was thinking. And when they landed in Dallas, she gave him no opportunity to find out. Murmuring she'd have to rush to make it to her office in time for her first appointment, she headed into the terminal, suitcase in tow. Watching her go, he felt desire clawing at him with a sharpness he'd never experienced before.

Brent knew he'd had no choice last night but to accept that unnamed issues over her ex-fiancé prompted her to pull back from involving herself with *him*. Even so, that didn't make him want her less. Or prevent him from imagining how her skin might have felt while his hands explored every subtle curve of her body.

It was just his bad luck that he'd had to deadhead from Dallas to Charlotte in a Cessna filled with a faint trace of Hope's unforgettable perfume. Her scent had tortured his system during the entire flight and kept her firmly in the forefront of his thoughts.

Now, three days later, he completed a preflight inspection of the Skylane, climbed into the cockpit and swore her scent still lingered there.

"The woman's haunting me," he grated through his teeth as he stabbed on his sunglasses against the bright rays of early morning sun.

He ran through the preflight procedures, checking each item off on a list on his clipboard. He knew this routine by heart, he could do it in his sleep, but he never relied on his memory alone; one moment of distraction, and he might miss something crucial. When he was soaring a few miles high was the wrong time to discover something wasn't working.

He started the engine and listened to the thrum as it caught and smoothed out. Next, he surveyed the instrumentation display, ensuring that all the data was normal. He idled the plane away from the FBO tie-down lot toward the chain-link gate on the airside area of the private terminal in which his office was located.

His upcoming flight had been spur of the moment, prompted by an urgent predawn call from his brother. Adam hadn't given many details, just that sudden trouble with an engine necessitated Ethan Hunt, along with his brother, Jared—an engine troubleshooter—to fly to the manufacturer's plant in order to get to the bottom of the problem.

With this weekend's race in New Hampshire being the first in the Chase for the NASCAR Sprint Cup, Brent knew that the Sanford Racing team's complete focus should be on preparations for the race. A crew chief taking a day off-site to deal with an engine issue at this point in the season spoke volumes about how urgent the problem was. Adam's hiring Jared Hunt, who some referred to as an "engine whisperer," to consult just underlined that urgency. So much so that Brent had called Randall Paris, one of the part-time pilots he kept on retainer, and lined him up to take the charter to Colorado Brent had been scheduled to fly that morning.

Just as he taxied in sight of the terminal building, he saw the rear door swing open and two men step out. Brent braked the plane in the parking area, then glanced over, verifying that the dark-haired men now striding toward the fence's gate were his passengers.

A heavy sense of inevitability settled in on him as he cut the plane's engine and climbed out onto the tarmac. Flying Hope Hunt's brothers around was guaranteed to keep her—and the kiss they'd shared—rooted in his thoughts. Good thing for him, neither brother had a clue about the lust-filled thoughts and lurid dreams he had about their sister.

When he'd first met Hope, it had struck him that she shared the same mouth shape and similar jawline as Ethan. Jared, too, he now realized as the engine expert stepped through the chain-link gate. That's where the resemblance ended between her and her half brothers, though. Hope's eyes were gray, not blue, and she stood just a little over five feet tall, while Ethan and Jared both topped six feet.

Ethan offered his hand, his face tight with strain. "Adam said you juggled your schedule to fly us this morning. Appreciate that." If the man had any qualms about flying with a former driver who'd left the NASCAR circuit under less than favorable conditions, he didn't let them show.

"No problem," Brent said, returning the handshake. "Hopefully this trip will get your engine problem solved." He shifted to shake hands with Jared. "The weather looks clear all the way."

"Good to hear," Jared replied.

Both men carried briefcases that they opted to keep with them instead of stowing in the luggage compartment. They also chose to settle in the plane's backseat so they could look over notes and test results during the flight.

While Brent buckled himself in, then fired up the engine, Ethan and Jared donned headsets so they could easily converse. Brent changed the frequency on his headset to the ATIS. The automated weather report hadn't changed since he'd checked it earlier.

He jotted down the data, then tuned the radio to the ground frequency and called ground control. Soon, he received clearance to taxi from the terminal to one of the runways.

The takeoff went smooth. The morning sun hit the windshield, warming the interior of the plane.

For the next hour, Brent focused on flying. He was aware of the men in the backseat conversing with each other, but he'd turned the volume down on his headset so their voices were a mere backdrop to the engine's thrum.

Then he heard Jared ask his brother how Hope was doing.

With studied nonchalance, Brent reached and turned up his headset's volume. Okay, so maybe he shouldn't eavesdrop, but he couldn't help it. The woman didn't just intrigue him, there was something more about her that drew him in ways no other woman had in a very long time. In the past, a female telling him she didn't want to get involved would have earned a shrug before he moved on down the road to greener pastures. But where Hope Hunt was concerned, the last thing he wanted to do was walk away. He didn't know why, but he damn well intended to find out. If eavesdropping on a conversation got him some answers, so be it.

"...Dad said the only time she's mentioned her ex was when he asked if Preftakes is still in prison," Ethan replied.

Brent frowned. Hope's ex-fiancé had wound up in prison? No wonder she had certain issues with the guy. But what did they have to do with her getting involved with *him*?

"She assured Dad that he's still locked up," Ethan added. "Which is a good thing, in my opinion. Otherwise, Dad would probably try to hunt him down so he could smash in his face for hurting Hope. Not to mention all those other women."

"I might just be tempted to give Dad a hand with that," Jared said.

"If you think you're going to get to hammer the guy without me going along with you, think again," Ethan informed him.

Hurting Hope and other women. Had Preftakes turned out to be some sort of sex criminal? Brent wondered. A murderer, maybe?

He bit back on frustration when the brothers' conversation switched back to the engine problem that had prompted their trip. And stayed there until they reached their destination.

To Brent's growing aggravation, neither man mentioned their sister or her incarcerated ex during the return flight to Charlotte.

Fine, he decided. He wasn't scheduled to pick up

Hope for three days. That should give him plenty of time to find out what Preftakes had done.

And exactly what past issues Hope had referred to as the reason she didn't want to get involved with *him*.

"So, you're calling this future get-together of my employees a morale-athon?" Seated in the chair in front of Hope's desk, Travis Watkins fanned through the leather-bound proposal she'd presented him.

"That's right," she replied.

"Isn't that the equivalent of saying the people who work for me are unhappy?" The businessman was large, not especially tall, but wide and portly. Hope suspected people tended to write him off as a hearty old fat man until they got a look at his smile. It reminded her of a shark's.

"Mr. Watkins, you recently acquired a company referred to by its employees as 'The Slave Pit.' The CEO kept a grenade on his desk. A large number of their coworkers were fired out of the blue and morale was flat. Then you come along, buy the company and suddenly their old jobs fall under your global tech conglomerate. They now have to blend in with your existing workforce that crosses languages and cultural divides. That's a lot of change to deal with in a short amount of time. It isn't going to be easy on anyone for a while."

A crafty gleam settled in Watkins's eyes. "Guess I knew that when I hired you to come up with the mother of all team-building plans," he said, his pure Texas drawl conjuring up images of wide blue skies and land dotted with longhorn cattle.

"I'd wager you've made it your business to know exactly how all of your employees feel," she said.

When she slid a discreet look at the small clock on

one corner of her neat-as-a-pin desk, she felt her stress level ratchet up. Her secretary had buzzed fifteen minutes ago to let her know Brent had arrived as planned and that he'd made a point to remind her they needed to leave for the airport ASAP so they could avoid Dallas's heavy afternoon flight traffic.

Hope had a mental image of him shooting his watch frustrated looks while he paced her reception room. Without warning, that image changed to one of his face inches from hers, his breath hot against her cheek.

No, she told herself, even as desire pooled deep in her belly. She had spent the past days convincing herself that her reaction to his kiss had been a fluke. After all, two years had passed since a man had touched her. It was only natural that her physical response to Brent Sanford had been over-the-top.

Curling her fingers into her palms, she reminded herself that she was a professional. She dealt in orderly, logical processes. All she needed to do was practice a little self-control.

Which is what she hoped Brent was doing in regard to having to wait on her. Travis Watkins was heart-stoppingly rich, and if he gave her proposal a green light, Hunt Consultants would have a chance to show the business community it was at the top of its game. No way would she suggest to one of the most successful entrepreneurs in Texas that he needed to vamoose so she could fly off to deal with Sanford Racing's personnel problems.

"I went over the main points of the proposal during my presentation," she said. "But I'm sure you'll want to read all of the documentation I've provided before you make a decision on whether you want to go forward with this project. My business card with my contact information is inside the proposal's cover. Just let me know if you have any questions."

"The only question I have is when can you start?"

Excitement shot through her veins like a potent drug, but she managed to keep her expression neutral. "My assistant will contact yours first thing in the morning to coordinate dates and locations."

"Sounds like a plan."

While Watkins hefted his bulky body out of the chair, Hope rose from hers, stepped around the desk and offered him her hand.

"Thank you, Mr. Watkins. I look forward to working with you and your staff."

"And I'm looking forward to your getting my new employees on the right track."

"I'll do my best."

She opened the door, gesturing for him to precede her into the reception area decorated with leather furniture, polished brasses and earth-toned area rugs. She had modeled the room after her father's cozy, masculine study that for her was the epitome of peaceful, secure surroundings.

Following Watkins out, Hope noted that her secretary had stepped away from her desk. Her gaze shifted to Brent as he turned from examining the contents in one of the floor to ceiling display shelves that lined the opposite wall.

He was dressed in pilot mode—starched white shirt, sedate black tie and dark slacks. The afternoon sun streaming through a window behind her secretary's desk put glints of gold in his dark eyes. Eyes that remained impassive as his gaze locked with hers.

Just the sight of him made Hope's mouth water and wedged a huge ball of emotion in her throat. A wave of sensation swept over her.

"Sorry to hold you up from your next appointment," Watkins said, nodding Brent's way.

"It's not a problem," Hope assured him. For her, anyway. Brent probably had a far different opinion of their delay in leaving for the airport.

The businessman tucked the leather binder holding her proposal under one arm, then strode over to Brent and offered his hand. "You've got a fine woman there, son. You'd be smart to keep a hold of her."

Mortification sent scalding heat up Hope's throat. Had her gaze been so transparent that Watkins had seen the war of emotions going on inside of her?

"Oh, we're not…" She lifted a hand, let it drop. "Mr. Watkins, this is Brent Sanford. He's a pilot, here to pick me up, is all."

Brent returned the man's handshake. "We're not," his voice sounded as dry as the desert when he echoed her words.

Watkins's shrugged. "I sure read that wrong." He gave Hope a nod before he disappeared out the door.

Easing out a slow breath, she ran a hand over the hip of her gray flannel slacks. "Brent, I apologize that my appointment ran late. But I couldn't ask Mr. Watkins to leave before we'd finished our business."

Brent looked at her steadily. "So, how'd the appointment go?"

"Wonderful." She couldn't help but send him a beaming smile. "Mr. Watkins's company has a global presence, so I'll be conducting team-building seminars overseas, too."

"Good for you." Brent stuck his hands in his pockets, his face remaining calm and expressionless. "I got the message from my office manager that you want to fly to New Hampshire instead of Charlotte."

His voice was as cool as the look in his eyes.

"That's right. I need to do some work with the pit crew. I thought I could do that in Charlotte, since they normally don't fly in until the morning of the race. But there's a charity pit crew challenge tomorrow at the New Hampshire track, so they're flying there today."

Brent gave a curt nod. "Ready to head to the airport?"

It didn't take the training she'd had in human behavior for her to understand what was going on. She had let him know in no uncertain terms she wasn't interested in developing a physical relationship with him. He had apparently accepted that, taken hold of his emotions and locked them away somewhere.

Hope lifted her chin. So, why hadn't she been able to do the same thing instead of spending the past days struggling against waves of desire? And why the heck did it now scratch at her pride for him to act like he'd never even kissed her?

His doing so simply made what might have been an uncomfortable situation bearable, she reminded herself. She and Brent Sanford were oil and water, with moral codes that in no way meshed. Yet, during one bout of sleeplessness, she'd gone online and researched him. It had been her intent to read all the information on what had been dubbed the *Fuelgate scandal* in order to shore up her defenses against him. But she'd found an article about something Brent had done after he left NASCAR racing and started his air charter operation that didn't jibe with her concept of the type of man who would bribe a gas man to sabotage a competitor.

What she'd learned about him didn't matter, Hope reminded herself. Every person's behavior exhibited inconsistencies from time to time. The bottom line was, their kiss had been a huge mistake, and she should be thankful Brent wasn't putting pressure on her for a repeat performance.

No matter how explosive it might be.

Dammit, she couldn't stop her gaze from dropping to his mouth. That firm, generous mouth. An ache, similar to longing, tried to expand inside of her. She ruthlessly tamped it down. She hadn't felt this off balance since the police showed up at her condo and arrested her fiancé.

She had detested the feeling then, and she didn't like it now.

Her gaze transferred to the entry door as it swung open. Her secretary—auburn-haired and pleasingly plump—stepped inside, a stack of file folders resting in the crook of one arm.

Grateful that her assistant's presence had jarred her out of her thoughts, Hope returned Brent's benign look.

"I've held you up long enough. I'll grab my purse and suitcase from my office, and we'll be ready to go."

FOR A SHRINK, HOPE HUNT SURE as hell had a sorry sense about people.

Brent had been gnawing on that thought for the past three days. He continued to chew on it as they left her office for the small general aviation airport in Dallas. It weighed on his mind while he did his preflight check, then took off. Now, halfway to New Hampshire, the frustrated anger he felt was as strong as it had been when he'd gone online and dug up the details on Hope's ex-fiancé.

David Preftakes had been an oil and gas broker who'd used his reportedly considerable charm to scam wealthy Texas widows by selling them shares in off-shore drilling rigs that didn't exist. The snake had conned his clients, business associates, family. And his fiancée, who had no doubt been mortified when the cops hauled him off from her condo in handcuffs. The guy had deserved to go to prison.

Brent understood why Hope might be gun-shy when it came to dropping her guard and getting involved in another relationship.

But she had told him she didn't want to get involved because the situation with her ex had made her cautious about certain *issues*. All of Brent's instincts zapped his brain with the message of exactly what those issues were. She intended to avoid hooking up with another man who wasn't above cheating in order to get what he wanted.

A man like *him*.

Only problem was, he hadn't tried to cheat anyone. But Hope had made her mind up about him from other people's say-so. Without any proof, she'd decided he was just like that conning bastard, Preftakes.

What the hell kind of psychologist made absolute judgments of someone she didn't know?

Brent tightened his fingers on the controls against the vicious case of angry frustration that had plagued him since he'd figured out what Miss Sunshine's *issues* were. He damn well didn't need that. Didn't need her. Didn't *want* a woman who was so narrow-minded.

Forget it, he ordered himself. Forget her and move on.

He slid a sideways look toward the passenger seat.

She was in full navigator mode, gripping a map in one hand while craning her neck to look out the window to check for points of reference.

Her dark hair was tucked behind her ear so he had a clear view of her throat. It was long and slender, circled by pearls that in the glow of the late afternoon sun made her skin seem only more delicate. He could smell her cool, quietly sexual scent over everything else.

And, dammit, the want for her was a great deal more personal than he'd bargained for. No matter how hard he tried to convince himself the opposite was true, her opinion of him mattered. He didn't want it to. Didn't want *her* to matter, but she did.

Caring for her made everything a huge study in frustration. But he *did* care, and the last thing he wanted to do was move on. So he was going to have to figure out what to do about that. About her.

"Why psychology?" he asked.

She swivelled her head his way, her brows peeking over the top of her sunglasses. "What?"

He reached, turned up the volume on her headset.

"While I was waiting in your office, I saw several plaques in the display case," he said. "They were awards for various things associated with your business. Meaning, you've scored some awards for being good at what you do. Why did you decide to be a psychologist?"

"Curiosity." The coolness in her voice didn't surprise him—he figured he deserved the same treatment he'd given her. And the silence that followed.

"To find the answers to all those questions people carry around in their heads?" he prodded.

WHAT WAS THE DEAL? HOPE wondered. From the moment she'd seen him in her office, he'd spoken only when necessary. Why did he suddenly want to talk?

She considered giving him the standard "I like helping people" response. But the wall of polite coolness he had erected between them had unnerved her. She didn't want to admit that, but it did. Just the fact that he for some reason had decided to end the uncomfortable silence uncurled something inside of her.

She laid the map in her lap. With her headset on, the sound of the engine was a muted hum in her ears. "My mother. I became a psychologist because of her."

"Did she need therapy?"

"Maybe. I'm not sure. We were close, and I could tell there was some deep-seated unhappiness or regret she was dealing with. Over the years I asked her several times what was wrong. She would always deny that something was bothering her. But then she'd get really quiet, and I knew that wasn't the truth. I wanted so much to help her, I just didn't know how."

"So, you learned. Became a psychologist."

"Too late. She died last year and I still don't know what it was that she kept secret for so long." Hope heard the quaver that the unremitting ache of losing her mother had put in her own voice. "I don't think I'll ever know."

"I'm sorry, Hope. That's got to be rough." Even through her headset, Brent's voice was soft, as intimate as the caress of his fingers had been against her flesh.

While a myriad of emotions swept through her, she shifted her gaze out the window, wishing the general aviation airport in Concord was nearer. For a man she was determined to avoid, she was too aware of everything about him. Too close to him physically and emotionally.

"I remember seeing my mother sad plenty of times while I was growing up," he said. "But I didn't have to wonder why she was unhappy. It was right there in front of her face. In front of everybody's face."

"Your father?" Hope ventured, remembering what Ethan had told her about the man who'd founded Sanford Racing.

"Yeah. His nickname was Wild Bobby. He loved racing and racy women. Didn't put much effort in keeping the latter a secret."

"That had to have been hard for your mother. And on you and your brothers."

"When we were little, she tried to protect us from all the rumors about Dad's messing around. But when Adam, Trey and I got older, we heard. And there was no way of keeping things quiet when he died while on a fishing excursion with his longtime mistress. That was ten years ago, and my mother still won't talk about it."

"Sometimes there are hurts so deep that you never get over them."

He checked the plane's gauges, noted all readings were as they should be. "Is that Dr. Hunt talking now?"

"That's all of me talking."

She shifted in her seat and looked at him. The casual pilot attire, the dark, bad-boy sunglasses suited him. She'd thought once that she knew exactly what kind of man he was. Now, she wasn't so sure.

"What?" he asked when he noticed her staring at him.

"I read something about you on the Internet."

His mouth tightened and she saw his shoulders tense

beneath his starched white shirt. "I drove in NASCAR races. There's a lot about me online. Good and bad."

"This wasn't something bad, and it didn't have anything to do with NASCAR. It happened after you stopped racing. While you were flying."

His forehead furrowed. "What?"

"You flew six men who were participating in a parachuting competition. The first five jumped from the plane successfully, but when the sixth tried to leap out and open his chute, it only partially deployed. The parachute lines got caught on—" she lifted a hand "—something on the plane."

"The twin propeller engine's undercarriage."

"You were at three thousand feet. Witnesses on the ground said they could see a body dangling from the plane. Everyone interviewed assumed the airplane would have to touch down with the man trapped underneath, and that he would surely be killed. But all of a sudden, the parachutist became free of the plane and was able to open his reserve chute and jump safely. That's because the pilot left his seat for about thirty seconds to reach out and cut the parachute lines that were caught."

Brent raised a shoulder. "That was the only option."

"No," Hope countered. "The article said you could have landed safely with the man still strapped to the plane. But instead, 'the pilot showed significant bravery and skill by risking his own life to save the man.'"

"It was more knee-jerk reaction than heroics. I was running low on fuel and didn't have a lot of time to think things through."

And didn't sound at all like a man who would put his

own interests first in any circumstance. Including when it came to winning a NASCAR race.

But he *had* done that. There was the gas man's sworn statement, plus videotape from the bar of him and Brent together. The cash deposited to the gas man's bank account. And, most telling, Brent had quit racing right after that.

"So, why?" he asked.

"Why what?"

"Why did you go online and check me out?"

"I told you, I'm curious about things."

"So you did." He gave her a long, intense look. "You're not the only one whose curiosity got the better of them."

"How so?"

"I checked you out online, too."

"How do you like my Web site?"

"Classy. Professional. I dug deeper than your Web site, though. Found some articles about your ex-fiancé."

Hope felt her own shoulders stiffen. "That's not an episode in my life that I enjoy revisiting."

"I don't blame you. But you don't have to revisit it. Just listen while I talk."

"All right."

"You had a slick con man take you for a ride, and you see me the same way you view him. Which makes me the last man you want to have anything to do with."

"Do you blame me?"

"For being gun-shy, no. But you've believed everything you've heard about me. I was *accused* of a lot of things, Hope. All of the evidence was circumstantial."

"Are you saying you didn't bribe that gas man to doctor the fuel in a competitor's race car?"

"That's exactly what I'm saying."

"Then why didn't you try to clear your name? Why did you just walk away from racing?"

"It didn't take me long to realize there was no way to clear my name. And if I'd stayed in racing, it would have hurt my family's business. What sponsor would have touched me after that? Or any other driver associated with Sanford Racing while I was still there? If I hadn't cut all ties, my family's business would have gone under."

She rubbed at an ache that had settled in her right temple. Why did he have to make such sense?

"You're afraid of getting hurt, I understand that," he continued while he reached to adjust a dial on the dash. "Who isn't?"

"This coming from a man who drove race cars at one hundred eighty miles an hour. You risked your own life by leaving the controls of an airplane to save that parachutist. You've lived on the edge and taken risks. I doubt you're afraid of anything."

"That's where you're wrong, Doc. I'm afraid that the first woman who's held my interest in a very long time is going to slam the door in my face. That she won't let herself get to know me and make up her own mind about who I am."

Hope sent up thanks that she was sitting down, because her legs were trembling. A man who could turn her into a quavering mass with just his words was every bit as dangerous as a loaded gun.

And she had no intention of taking a stray bullet.

But, Lord, she thought, Brent Sanford sure had a way about him.

A way of looking at her out of those fabulous dark eyes as if she were the sole focus of his universe. A way of talking to her with that smooth sexy voice as if he'd waited his whole life to speak to her. A way of touching her with those clever hands so that a simple brush against her flesh tied her in knots.

He was making her crazy, and she knew full well she didn't have the option of going down that road.

Still, she couldn't deny that what he'd said was true—she'd let her experience with her ex influence how she viewed him. And judged his involvement in the Fuelgate Scandal on media reports and word of mouth.

She thought about the little boy Brent had gone out of his way to find a toy NASCAR race car for. About the parachutist who was alive because Brent had risked his own life to save the man.

Taking all that into account only added to the mass of confusion she found herself tangled in. "I don't know…what to say."

"You don't have to say anything. Just think about giving me a chance. *Us* a chance."

Hope shifted her gaze to the windshield, spotted the runway of the small Concord, New Hampshire, airport.

Over her headset, she heard Brent contact the tower on the radio and was cleared to land.

He wouldn't be coming to the race track this week. Trey Sanford was off medical leave and scheduled to drive in the Sprint Cup Series race. Since she planned to go to Charlotte after the race, Adam had reserved a seat for her on the team's plane. There would be no reason for her to see Brent again until next week.

That should give her plenty of time to get her thoughts into some kind of order.

At least she hoped it would.

"I'll think about what you said," she agreed.

Out of the corner of her eye, she saw his mouth curve. That hard, firm mouth. She closed her eyes, knowing she would think about little else.

CHAPTER SEVEN

THE FOLLOWING MORNING, a chilly little breeze cooled the September sunshine, so Hope paired her jeans and long-sleeved-shirt sporting the Sanford Racing team's logo with a leather jacket.

Today was the day that teams began to practice and qualify—hopefully!—in order to take part in the actual race on Sunday. Qualifying meant showing that a car was not just fast, but fast enough. To do so, a driver had to complete at least one full-speed lap around the track without crashing or losing control of his car. Qualifying set the race's starting lineup and, if there were more cars attempting to qualify than the forty-three allowed in each race, weeded out the slowest.

Hope remembered hearing her father talk about the New Hampshire race track. It had sharp turns, long straightaways, and it was *one-groove*, meaning there was only one part of the track where a car's tires got the best grip. Move out of that groove, and the car became less stable and harder to control, which made passing other cars difficult.

Qualifying well allowed a driver to start the race up front. That way, he or she could avoid having to pass a large number of cars during the race, which was especially important at the New Hampshire track.

Practice time on the track enabled the race teams to tinker with their cars to provide an extra burst of speed for that oh-so-important qualifying lap. A huge amount of the tinkering was already going on when Hope walked past the garage stalls that had been assigned to the various teams.

The roar of engines being tested and tuned was intense. As was the smell of burnt oil and high octane fuel. Beneath the soles of her tennis shoes she could feel the ground tremble. The air felt electric with the anticipation that surrounded every practice and qualifying round.

The inhabitants of the garage stalls were too busy to even look up as she walked by. Crew members with credentials hanging from lanyards darted between the garage and the big haulers parked nearby, their chrome surfaces reflecting the strengthening morning sunlight. In almost every stall she passed, tables held computer monitors, printers and other electronic devices. Groups of people stared at the data streaming across the screens.

She found Trey Sanford's No. 483 car parked in a stall at the very end of the building. The Greenstone Garden Centers blue-and-yellow logo painted on the trunk lid made the dark blue car impossible to miss. The front end of the vehicle was jacked up off the ground, one of its tires missing. Two men stood near the front, peering into the engine compartment.

She spotted Ethan at the driver's side of the car, talking to Trey who was dressed in his uniform. She had met Trey last night when their paths crossed at the pit crew competition that had been held to benefit several charities. As she had then, she was struck by his resemblance to Brent. Granted, Brent was several inches taller and his hair a darker brown than Trey's, but they had the same chiseled features and strong profiles.

Just looking at Trey made her miss his older brother. Hope closed her eyes. She hadn't stopped thinking about what Brent had said during their flight to New Hampshire. Hadn't been able to erase his soft, compelling words from her memory.

Or calm the churning in her nerves that just the prospect of letting down her guard and getting emotionally—and physically—involved with him had settled inside her.

Once upon a time, she would have simply told him she wasn't interested. Period. But she wasn't into lying, not even to herself, and she knew she needed to take a good long look at the attraction she seemed to be developing. Okay, the attraction she had *already* developed.

Where Brent was concerned, she was sorely tempted to throw caution to the wind and just let herself feel. But she'd done that once before, and gotten her heart broken by a man who was in no way what he seemed to be on the surface.

Back then, she'd been realistic enough to accept that there would be other men in her future. *The far distant future.* Even so, she'd sworn to herself that she would never again put emotion over reason. Never again be fooled by a handsome face and charmer's grin.

Had Brent been set up to take the fall in the Fuelgate scandal as he claimed? Or, like her ex, did he have a talent for telling exorbitant lies while maintaining an innocent expression so compelling it had the power to draw people in?

That she had no way of truly knowing made Hope feel as if she was standing on a fault line, waiting for the earthquake. No lie detector test was handy to let her know if Brent had told the truth. Nor did she have any way to judge his intent where she was concerned.

She'd been trained to look at other people's lives, analyze the pros and cons, then diagnose. But when it came to her own life and the decision she now faced, her objectivity had flown out the window. It seemed impossible to separate whatever tangled strands of truth were mixed in with speculation.

It didn't help that she could still feel the imprint of his mouth on hers. Still taste him.

No, Hope told herself, clamping down on emotion. She needed to think with her head, not her heart.

The good news was, she had time to sort things out. She wouldn't see Brent for over a week when he was scheduled to fly her to the race in Delaware. Hopefully she would have a few things figured out by then.

The sudden shriek of an air wrench jerked Hope out of her thoughts.

She shifted her gaze back to the front of the car. Its tire had been replaced and it was now off the jack. The hood was closed. The dark blue car looked ready to roll beneath the row of fluorescent lights.

Ethan's headset hung half on and half off one side of his head while he talked to Trey. His expression serious, Trey said a few words, then turned and climbed through the window of his car.

Luis Macha scurried over and handed Trey's helmet through the window. The team's front tire carrier looked as tense today as he had at last week's race when his fumbling a tire resulted in a pit stop taking a few seconds longer than it should have.

Last night, Luis and his fellow over-the-wall team

members had done well in the charity competition, so they'd left to celebrate before Hope had a chance to get him alone for a chat. She intended to do that as soon as she saw an opening.

She watched Trey slip on his helmet, then his leather driving gloves. The car's starter chugged for an instant before the boom of all eight pistons roared through the garage. A couple of guys stepped up and pushed the car backward. After it cleared the garage, the vehicle lurched forward and the No. 483 car headed toward the track for a few practice rounds.

She looked back at Luis in time to see him pull a cell phone off the waistband of his pants. He answered the call while heading out the door.

Hope caught up with him just outside the building where he'd stopped beside a huge, wheeled toolbox. She waited to step forward until he finished his call.

"Hi, Luis, how are you doing?"

He turned at the sound of her voice. His dark eyes swept over her, then instantly flicked across her shoulder, as if he were expecting to see someone.

"Fine," he said, his gaze returning to her. His brown hair looked windblown, and his massive arms in the team polo shirt gave the impression he could bench-press the race car Trey Sanford had just driven away in.

"I was at the competition last night," Hope said. "You and your team did great."

"Didn't win."

During her initial interview with Luis, he had given short, succinct answers to every question she'd asked. She had no expectation he would all of a sudden turn chatty on her.

"Coming in third isn't so bad," she pointed out. "I'm

just wondering how things are going now that Trey is off medical leave."

"We'll know more after he qualifies."

Standing only inches from the massive toolbox, Hope felt the sun radiating heat off of its silver-painted surface. "Actually, I wasn't referring to Trey's driving. I'm wondering how you're handling the fact that you had to sign a confidentiality agreement not to discuss his medical condition."

"Since NASCAR'S okay with it, so am I." Luis raised a shoulder. "It's the man's own business whether or not to go public."

"Are you satisfied with everything else? Do you have any issues with how the team's run?"

"I didn't."

"Didn't?" Hope asked, picking up on his use of the past tense.

"Up until last week, things were fine."

"What happened last week?"

"Brent Sanford showed up at the track."

Hope felt a jolt of surprise, but kept her expression benign. "Why did his coming to watch the race make you feel things were no longer fine?"

"Four years ago, he disgraced the team."

Hope had done some digging and discovered the personnel file she'd been given for Luis showed only his *recent* employment with Sanford Racing. He'd worked there the first time during the Fuelgate scandal, but his old file had been put in storage when he'd quit shortly thereafter, and a clerical error had caused it to be overlooked when he was rehired several months ago. "Is what Brent Sanford was accused of the reason you quit your job with Sanford Racing back then?"

"I don't like being associated with anything to do with cheating."

"But you came back to work for the company."

"I've got a wife and kid to support. Adam Sanford pays good wages and I like working for the man. But I won't be here long if his brother gets involved with the team again in any way."

"Is his brother's showing up at the race last week the reason that last pit stop didn't go smoothly?"

Luis's gaze narrowed on her and his mouth set in a hard line. "I know you're working for the boss, but that doesn't mean I need to be analyzed." He crammed his cell phone back onto his waistband. "I gotta get back to the garage."

"Talk to you later." Hope watched him stalk off, his beefy hands curled into fists.

"Interesting," she murmured. She understood why Luis—why anyone—would have a problem being associated with a team whose driver had been accused of sabotaging a competitor's car. But Brent had immediately quit racing and walked away from his family's business. He'd founded his charter service and it was well-known he'd made a success of his own business. It wasn't as if there was talk that he might somehow try to return to the racing circuit.

Still puzzling over Luis's strong reaction to Brent showing up to watch a race four years after the fact, Hope returned to the garage area.

There, she was pleased to see Adam Sanford conferring with two of the team's mechanics. From talking to Adam's secretary, she knew his schedule leading up to this weekend's race was filled with sponsor-related events. Greenstone Garden Centers had been nervous about Trey missing the past two races. Although Shelly Green's good finishes in those races had helped, Adam intended to make sure the sponsor stayed committed one-hundred percent to both Trey and Sanford Racing.

Even so, Adam had carved time out of his schedule to come to the garage and touch base with his team. Hope felt satisfied she had convinced him that rebuilding his employees' morale and trust wouldn't happen without a close-knit, full-on effort in which every person—from the owner to the catch can man to the floor sweeper—was acknowledged as having a vital role to play and respected for their contribution. Adam's continued presence was the starting point for some great synergy developing among the team members. But he still had work to do. Hope made a mental note to recommend to Adam that he pay particular attention to Luis Macha.

As if he felt her gaze on him, Adam looked in her direction. He raised a hand, indicating he wanted to talk to her. Hope paused beside a fuel cart holding three gas cans. She felt overshadowed by the rocket-red cans that from their bottom to the end of their spouts matched her height.

"Hope, how are things going?" Adam asked when he strode over to her. The man exuded authority even in his team polo shirt and faded blue jeans.

"Fine. There's a personnel issue I'd like to discuss with you, but it can wait until after the race. How are Trey's practice laps going?"

"Fine, so far. We had a problem earlier in the week with an engine part. I had to shanghai Brent at the last minute to fly both of your brothers to the engine manufacturer. We're keeping our fingers crossed that the steel part they made to replace a faulty aluminum one does the trick."

"I'll keep mine crossed, too."

"Are you still planning on flying back to Charlotte on the team plane after the race on Sunday?"

"Yes. I'll be available to work with your guys all next week." Hope paused. "Is my flying on your plane a problem?"

"No, but I do have a problem. It has to do with Brent. Since you'll be in Charlotte next week, I'm hoping you can help me out."

At the mention of Brent's name, she felt an instant, gnawing curiosity. "What do you need me to do?"

"His birthday is Wednesday and our mother has spent weeks planning a surprise party for him. She's got a room booked at a museum. Your sister's doing the catering."

"Sounds like quite a to-do."

"It will be if we can get the guest of honor to show up. In the years since he quit racing, Brent's avoided a lot of family get-togethers."

"I'd think that would be a time when he needed his family."

"Long story." Adam shoved his fingers through his dark hair. "Anyway, it's almost guaranteed that if Brent gets wind that something's being planned for his birthday, he'll make a point to schedule some cross-country charter flight and be unavailable. I don't want our mother disappointed. I told her I thought you could maybe help."

Hope blinked. "Me?"

"There's no reason for you to know when Brent's birthday is. That means he won't be suspicious if you ask him to do something."

"Like accompany me to some art exhibit at the museum?"

"Exactly." Adam frowned. "He's not too keen on arty stuff, so you might want to think of something else."

The roar of an engine had Adam glancing over his shoulder. Seconds later, Trey's car pulled into the garage stall. He'd barely stopped before the hood got popped and several men began hovering over the engine.

"I've got to talk to Trey, then get back with his sponsor," Adam said. "I'd appreciate it if you could figure out some way to get Brent to the party."

Adam seemed so harried that she didn't want to tell him no. "I'll think of something," Hope assured him.

"Change of plans," she muttered as Adam strode away. Since Wednesday would be here before she knew it, she was going to have to figure out what to do about having a relationship with Brent Sanford a heck of a lot sooner than she'd planned.

FOR THE FIRST TIME IN HIS LIFE, a woman had gotten under his skin and was driving him crazy, Brent thought as he steered his coal-black sports car through Charlotte's early evening traffic.

First, Hope had called, saying urgent business had come up with a client and asking him to meet her at the airport ASAP to fly her to Dallas. That, however, wasn't a problem—he was used to juggling his schedule. Clients often changed destinations, even cancelled charters at the last minute. Then there was the weather that occasionally wreaked havoc with everyone's agenda.

Just another day at the office.

He'd barely had time to pass the charter he'd been scheduled to fly to Lake Tahoe to one of his backup pilots when Hope called again. Could he pick her up at the Levine Museum because she had to drop off something to her sister, who was catering an event there? Fine. It didn't bother him to drive halfway across the city to pick her up.

What goaded him was that during both calls, she hadn't said one word about *them*.

Did she think it had been easy for him to admit he had feelings for her? he brooded as he maneuvered through the heavy traffic. Had she considered it a walk in the park for him to acknowledge he wanted a relationship to develop between them? Because she said she needed time to think he hadn't seen or talked to her since he flew her to New Hampshire. The least the woman could have done over the phone was *acknowledge* she was still thinking about what he'd said. Instead, she'd sounded efficient and businesslike, as if he'd never even brought up the subject.

Or if she'd maybe decided to pass on his offer.

Jaw set, he braked at a red light. Rapped his fingers against the steering wheel while the bluesy ache of a tenor sax poured out of the stereo. It was a sorry state for a man who'd once had women tumbling for him like bowling pins to realize the one woman he wanted just might not be interested.

Dammit, he wasn't anything like her bastard of an ex-fiancé. *He* hadn't cheated to try to win a NASCAR race. Any race for that matter. Why the hell couldn't she just take his word for that?

"Because she can't," he muttered as the signal light changed. *He* was the one who used to live his life in the fast lane. Every day. Every way. Hell, professionally he still did that, only now he buckled himself in behind the controls of a plane instead of a high-powered stock car.

Hope had been taken for a wild ride by a smooth con man. The last thing she would do is dive into another relationship when there were no doubt numerous warning signs blipping through her brain. It would be a matter of self-preservation for her to be cautious. To take things slow. To hold at arm's length a man she wasn't sure she could trust.

If that was the best he could get for now, so be it, Brent resolved. Problem was, he couldn't foresee things between them changing unless he somehow convinced her to trust him.

And just how was he going to pull that minor miracle off if he couldn't clear his name? Scowling, he conjured up the image of Mike Jones. Tall and muscular, the gas man had done a good job of putting all aspects of the setup into play that had effectively tanked the racing career of a driver with a good shot at winning that year's NASCAR Sprint Cup Series Championship.

Scowling, Brent whipped the sports car into the alley behind the museum. A few yards farther along he spotted a panel van with *Gourmet by Grace* scrolled across its side. Hope had told him to park in the loading zone beside her sister's catering van, then knock on the museum's back door and tell the security guard he was there to pick her up.

He climbed out of the car into the balmy evening air, rapped on the locked door. Moments later, it swung open to reveal a beefy uniformed security guard with a gray crew cut.

"I'm looking for Hope Hunt," Brent said. "She said she'd be waiting for me in the kitchen."

The guard checked a list of names on a clipboard, then pointed down a brightly lit corridor. "First door on the right," he said.

"Thanks." By the time Brent reached the kitchen, the

air was ripe with good, rich scents that made his mouth water. He thought back to when Tony Winters had shown up in his office for his flight to New York with a box of his sister-in-law's killer hors d'oeuvres. Wondering if Winters had snagged the job he'd interviewed for, Brent decided to try to get another sample of Grace's cooking before he and Hope left the museum.

He stepped through an open door into a brightly lit kitchen where several people dressed in white shirts and black slacks were busy loading flutes of champagne and a variety of hors d'oeuvres onto doily-covered silver trays. At the sound of heels clicking against the tile floor, he turned and spotted Hope heading his way.

Her dark hair was swept up and back, emphasizing her sculpted cheekbones. She wore a snug, short-skirted suit in traffic-stopping red with mile-high seductress heels in the same color.

Seeing her, just seeing her, made his chest go tight. "Hey, Doc."

"Hey, Captain Sanford." Smiling, she stepped forward and squeezed his arm, bringing with her the scent of some heady French perfume. "Thanks for agreeing to fly me to Dallas at the last minute. And for driving here to pick me up."

It occurred to him she was a little overdressed for a plane ride, but for all he knew she'd had a business meeting right before coming here. "All part of the service Sanford Aviation offers its navigators."

She tilted her head to the side. The dark red stones at her ears caught the light and glinted. "I didn't realize the job had so many perks."

Her lips were glossed with the same red as her suit,

and he wanted a taste of them—and a great deal more than that. "Speaking of perks, do you think we could abscond with some of your sister's hors d'oeuvres?"

"Grace always cooks extra, so I'm sure she can spare some. Why don't I introduce you to her and we'll ask?"

Brent glanced around the kitchen at the servers working at a frenetic pace. "She might be too busy for chitchat. Why don't we just swipe some hors d'oeuvres and head to the airport?"

"That would be rude. And the party Grace is catering won't get started in earnest until the guest of honor arrives." Hope tucked her hand into the curve of his arm and gave him a tug. "Come on, she's just down the hall making a last-minute check of the table setup."

Hope escorted him through a gallery where several illuminated pedestals displayed sculptures of colorful Venetian glass almost thin enough to read through. Subdued lights illuminated framed artwork hanging on the walls. Just beyond a staircase with a thick velvet rope strung across its base, she indicated an arched entryway to their right. "Grace is in there."

Her scent was clogging his brain. Each step he took beside her had him feeling more agitated and primitive enough to toss her over his shoulder and carry her off to some place where they could be alone. Dammit, he wanted her to at least acknowledge that he'd opened the door to his feelings for her. To admit that she owed him an answer. And if that answer was no, he was going to have to figure out a way to convince her to change her mind.

"We'll get to your sister in a minute." He nudged Hope into a small alcove just outside the arched doorway.

She gave a startled gasp as her hands locked on his upper arms. "Brent, what are you doing?"

"Talking to you. I have a question."

HOPE GAZED UP INTO HIS DARK, intense eyes, and instantly felt the heat moving up from her toes. She had to remind herself there were nearly fifty people waiting for him in the next room. The security guard would have already called Adam to tell him Brent had arrived. The candles on the cake had no doubt been lit.

"Your question can't wait until after I introduce you to Grace?" she asked. The erratic pounding of her pulse had turned her voice breathless.

"*I* don't want to wait." When one of his palms cupped the side of her throat, her legs began to tremble. "You told me you'd think about us."

She swept her tongue across her suddenly dry lips. "I kept my word."

"And?"

"And, we need to talk."

"I'm listening."

"Not here." Her lungs felt tight. She took a careful breath to clear them. "Not now."

"When?"

"Later."

He lowered his head, pressed his forehead against hers. "I haven't been able to think of anything but you for days, Doc. Got a name for that condition?"

Her nerves jittered in time with her pulse. "How about *obsession*?"

"Works for me. How about you tell me what we need to talk about?"

"I don't—"

"HEY, BRO, HOW ABOUT YOU unhand that gorgeous woman and let's get the show on the road?"

At the sound of his brother's voice, Brent expelled a soft oath and turned. "What the hell are you doing here?"

Trey Sanford shot him an unrepentant grin. The youngest Sanford brother wore a dark suit, but had left the collar of his crisp dress shirt unbuttoned and had forgone wearing a tie. "Making our mom happy."

"She sounded plenty happy when she called me early this morning to wish me a happy birthday before I flew a charter out of Nashville." Brent narrowed his eyes against the suspicion buzzing in his brain. "Tell me this isn't what I think it is."

"No can do, bro. Mom's wanted to give you a birthday bash for a couple of years, but you've always managed to sidestep her plans. Not this year. So, birthday boy, you need to act really surprised when you make an appearance in the room next door."

"Hell." Brent looked back at Hope. "Apparently, we're not flying to Dallas."

"Not tonight." She beamed him a bright smile. "Which means you can have all the hors d'oeuvres and champagne you want."

"Freaking ray of sunshine, aren't you?"

"I try to always look on the bright side." She patted his arm. "You'd better go in and make your mamma happy. Meanwhile, I'm going to slip into the kitchen. One of Grace's crew called in sick, so I promised I'd give her a hand."

"Oh, no, you don't." He clamped a hand around her wrist. "You got me here, Doc. That means I've got you for the entire night."

He felt a grim satisfaction when her pulse jumped against his palm. *"Entire?"* she asked.

"Oh, yeah," he said, tugging her close. "All. Night. Long."

CHAPTER EIGHT

FOR THE MOST PART, HOPE LOVED parties. Loved to dress up and spend an evening in a crowd. It didn't matter if she knew a single soul, as long as there were plenty of people, chilled drinks, music and interesting food.

And going stag had never presented a problem for a woman born with a gift for conversation. That, plus an inborn open friendliness, enabled her to entertain herself by mingling and moving from person to person and group to group.

Tonight, though, she spent at Brent's side. It wasn't just because he'd claimed that keeping her in close proximity would be payback for her part in getting him to the museum. Her own professional curiosity had joined in the mix.

From the instant his brother Trey showed up, she had noted the change in Brent's body language. Granted, some of the tension had surely been due to Trey interrupting her and Brent's encounter in the close confines of the alcove. Add to that Brent's learning he'd been trapped by well-meaning family and friends for a party in his honor. But Hope had sensed an extra tension going on between the two younger Sanford brothers.

A tension that hadn't been evident during the evening while she and Brent chatted with Adam and his sports biographer fiancée, Tara Dalton. Even when the subject turned to Tara's upcoming book on NASCAR's dynastic families and the interview Brent had given the author about the Fuelgate scandal. No, Hope thought, whatever it had been that caused Brent's shoulders to stiffen and his mouth to set in a thin line in Trey's presence had been due to some specific dynamics between himself and his younger brother.

The psychologist in her was still musing over that three hours into the party when Brent's office manager, Maureen Queen, coaxed him away to chat with the owner of the fixed base operation at the Charlotte airport. Deciding some fresh air would help her focus her thoughts, Hope stepped through the terrace doors that had been thrown open to allow the guests to spill out into the warm fall night.

There, Kath Sanford had just stepped away from conversing with one of Brent's backup pilots.

"Hope, I want to thank you again for arranging to get my son here tonight." Clad in a trim, coral-colored cocktail suit, the Sanford matriarch was tall with elegant posture and short hair a mixture of brown and soft gray. Her hazel-green eyes glinted in the glow of torches that had been positioned on the terrace to brighten the twilight.

"You're welcome, Mrs. Sanford. But I think Brent would use the word *connived* to describe how I managed to get him here."

"No doubt," Kath said, gesturing with the champagne flute she held in a narrow-boned hand. "But you got him here, and that's what counts. I haven't been able to pin him down to attend a large gathering of family and friends in a long time." A look crossed her face, a quick shadow. "Brent didn't just walk away from racing four years ago. On some level, he pulled emotionally away from the family."

"I'm sure that's been difficult."

"What's been difficult?" Brent asked as he joined them and handed Hope one of the champagne flutes he carried.

She angled her chin. In the flickering torchlight, the prominent planes of his face looked more rugged than refined. He belonged, she thought, on a billboard advertising high-end liquor or the kind of cars few could afford.

"Getting you here without your finding out about the party," she said lightly. "It was an extremely difficult process."

His mouth curled sardonically. "Maybe that's because I was lured here under false pretenses."

Hope sent him a somber look over the rim of her glass. "When dealing with individuals with behavioral problems, one must employ whatever methods are necessary."

"And it worked beautifully." Kath patted her son's arm. "Brent, you're not to blame Hope for her little ruse. She just seemed the best person available to get you here without your becoming suspicious. The main thing is that you appear to be having a good time."

He placed a hand over his mother's. "Tonight's psychologist in residence apparently believes I'm managing to behave myself." He shot Hope a long, simmering look that made her pulse stutter. "For now."

Kath studied Hope with apparent growing interest. "It does appear that the doctor has a positive effect on you." She glanced at a couple currently filling plates at the dessert buffet just inside the door. "There are several guests I still need to speak with, so you'll have to excuse me. I look forward to seeing you again soon, Hope."

"Thank you, Mrs. Sanford."

While his mother crossed the nearly deserted terrace, Hope turned her attention back to Brent. "Just so you don't wind up with a complex, I was kidding about the behavioral problems. You've been the perfect guest of honor. You didn't even flinch when the waiters rolled out the cart holding the birthday cake blazing with all those candles."

"Good thing Adam was nearby to help me blow them out."

She nodded slowly. "Trey was there, too. But you didn't gesture for him to help."

"So?"

"So, earlier when we were in the hallway and Trey showed up, I sensed a definite tension between you two."

"I was about to kiss you. My little brother screwed that up."

"I got the impression it was more than that."

Brent set his empty champagne flute on the top of the ledge that rimmed the terrace. "Sounds like I'm talking to Dr. Hunt now."

"You're speaking to a woman who is considering getting involved with you. She's simply wondering about your family dynamics."

"Considering," he repeated, his dark eyes sharpening. "What sort of considerations are involved here?"

She gazed up at him through her lashes. "That depends on several issues."

"Such as?"

"Your family dynamics being one. I'd like to know what's going on between you and Trey."

BRENT EASED OUT A SLOW BREATH. The moon was up now, and a mix of moonlight and torchlight turned her eyes to mesmerizing silver. He could tell her that what was between him and his younger brother was none of her business. But that wouldn't do anything about getting her to trust him. *Getting her.*

"What's between Trey and myself started out as pretty much friendly competition when we were teenagers. Our dad was a NASCAR Sprint Cup Series driver who believed in testing the rules. He wanted all of his sons to follow in his footsteps. Trey and I did."

"What about Adam? Did he want to be a driver, too?"

"No. He was always more interested in the business side of racing. Good thing, too, since Dad had little patience for budgets and board meetings."

"When did the friendly competition between you and Trey change?"

"It seemed to get more intense over time. Then things took a bad turn years ago during a big race when we caused each other to hit a wall. That knocked both of our cars out of the running. Afterward, Trey accused me of thumbing my nose at all rules. He said some day I'd be sorry for how I always pushed the envelope to get what I wanted."

"If you and Trey were trying to emulate your father, weren't you both guilty of doing that?"

"Trey didn't see it that way. I got the impression he thought I considered myself better than him, and was determined to prove it at all costs."

Hope set her empty flute aside. "Did you think that about yourself?"

"No. I viewed him as a worthy opponent who I wanted to beat, fair and square." Brent shifted his gaze. Beyond the edge of the terrace, the grounds of the museum were covered in a murky darkness. He wished that age-old rivalry was the only thing standing between him and his brother. "Trey also has his own opinion about what happened at Talladega."

"He believes you bribed the gas man to doctor the fuel?"

"He's never come out and said it. But I sensed when the scandal broke that he stood behind me only because our mother insisted the entire family close ranks."

"Have you talked to Trey about this?"

"Hell, no. You think I want to hear my baby brother tell me to my face that he thinks I'm scum? Talking to him about it would only make things between us worse."

"If you don't talk, things won't ever get better."

"I don't *want* to talk to Trey about it. This isn't something that can be fixed, Hope. No matter what I say, Trey will believe what he chooses."

"YOU MAY BE RIGHT. YOU COULD also be wrong."

"True." Brent reached out, took her hand. "Apparently, Dr. Hunt, you believe meaningful conversation can clear up a lot of things."

"I couldn't do my job if people refused to talk to me."

"What a coincidence," he said while threading his fingers through hers. "I have a certain matter I'd like to consult you about."

"What?"

"There's this woman who claims she's considering getting involved with me." Lifting her hand, he pressed his mouth to her knuckles and sent her nerves skittering. "But she keeps skirting the issue. Would you recommend a hands-on approach in this instance?"

"Sometimes…." Hope put her free hand to her temple. The champagne had made her pleasantly dizzy, and Brent's touch was doing crazy things to her pulse. "Sometimes…that type of approach can be effective."

"I like a lot of things about her." He leaned in, his mouth inches from her ear. "The way she smells." His lips grazed the side of her throat. "Challenging."

He was doing it to her again. Making her mind fuzzy, her skin shiver. If he kept this up, she wasn't going to present much of a challenge.

"Then there's her face, her hair, her mind." She felt his murmured words whisper along her skin and thrilled to them. "Her body," he added. "All so compelling. I don't know whether to bay at the moon or whimper at her feet. Which do you recommend?"

"Neither." She didn't want to play word games. She wanted to feel that wild sweep of pleasure that she knew from experience would come from the press of his mouth on hers. "Neither," she repeated, and slid her arms around his neck. "My professional opinion is that you should just kiss her."

"You're the doctor." He said it slowly, then moved like lightning to close his mouth over hers.

The kiss they'd shared before hadn't prepared Hope for the punch of this one. It was raw, and hot, and bulleted straight to her belly to leave her muscles quivering and nerve endings quaking.

She suddenly knew what it was like to go from zero to eighty, without having strapped herself in first.

She clamped her hands on his hips and let the speed take her.

The murmur of conversation from the guests just beyond the doors dimmed away. Her system was suddenly full of the scent of him instead of the heady aroma of the night.

She felt a churning deep inside of her. A frenzy. But the need sped beyond the lovemaking she knew instinctively they could share. She knew, if she let herself, she could fall for him all the way.

A man she didn't even know she could trust. Heaven help her, things weren't going the way she had planned!

A small jolt of panic had her pulling back. "Brent—"

"Not yet." He caught her face in his hands. He stared down at her.

"I…" Her voice hitched. "I need to catch my breath."

"All right." He let his hands fall from her face.

"I didn't intend for that to happen again." She took a step back. "Not for a while."

"Well, it did."

"Yes, it certainly did," she said on a long breath. "I didn't think I would have to give you an answer about our getting involved until next weekend when you fly me to the race in Dover. But then this party came up."

"Are you saying you need more time to consider things?"

She had thought maybe she did. But after the kiss they'd just shared…. A shiver worked up her spine, deliciously. "No, I've made a decision." And, Lord, help her, she hoped it was the right one.

"I'm listening."

"I'm interested." Still half-dazed, she gave her head a shake. "Obviously. But I need to take things slow. I was engaged to a man I thought I knew. Turns out, I didn't know him at all." She raised a hand, let it drop. "Slow might not appeal to a man used to fast cars and planes. And has been rumored to prefer fast women, too."

"Circumstances change, Hope. So do people. *You* appeal to me. Just you."

She saw the desire in his eyes and felt the raw echo of it sound through her. Keeping her hands off him was not going to be easy. Still, she was determined to guard her heart.

"If we're going to form any kind of relationship, I need us to be friends first."

"Friends." His eyes narrowed. "What sort of friends?"

"Friends…with benefits, sort of."

"Which means?"

"We date." She scraped her fingertips across her forehead. Her lips were still tingling from his. "Spend time together. Quality time so we can get to know each other. I need that before…well, anything else. I can't give you more than that right now. I'll understand if that isn't enough for you."

With one finger, he traced the curve of her jaw. "It'll have to be."

She was surprised to find herself torn between a sense of relief and a tingle of regret. But she knew she was right to toss up the walls. For now.

"So," she continued, "what you said about our spending tonight together—all night—is going to have to wait."

His mouth curved into a smile that was slow, very male, and should have required some kind of permit, considering the effect it had on her pulse.

"When we do get around to those things," he said softly, "we'll have to make sure they were worth waiting for."

A HALF HOUR LATER, HOPE SLID onto one of the long-legged stools in the museum's kitchen. She planted her elbows on the stainless steel island and looked at her sister, standing across the shiny expanse.

"Holy. Cow."

Grace Hunt Winters glanced up from the paperwork spread out in front of her. Like her employees, she wore a starched white shirt and black slacks. Her gleaming blond hair was pulled neatly back from her flawless face, anchored into a ponytail with a black velvet bow. She wore a gold band on her left ring finger, the sign of a commitment to the beloved husband who had drowned, leaving her with three small children to raise. "Holy cow, what?"

"I'm in trouble, Grace. Big trouble."

Instantly, concern shadowed her half sister's blue eyes. "What the heck happened? What kind of trouble?"

"The worst there is. Man trouble."

Grace's blond brows rose. "When you swore off men after your fiancé's arrest, I wasn't sure you'd ever want to get involved again."

"Learning that one's fiancé is a rat-faced liar has that sort of effect. And, for the record, I don't *want* to get involved with anyone." Hope furrowed her brow. "That doesn't seem to make any difference."

"Okay." Grace moved around the counter to stand at Hope's side. "Spill it. Who is he?"

"Brent Sanford."

Grace's eyes went wide. "*The* Brent Sanford? Tonight's guest of honor? The former NASCAR driver our father derides whenever his name comes up in a conversation?"

"You got it," Hope said. Like herself, Grace had grown up spending hours at race tracks with their crew chief father. After winning the Young Chef of the Year award, Grace went to work as the personal chef for a NASCAR driver. That gave her the opportunity to cook for celebrities from all walks of life, and led to a cooking show on TV that now played nationwide. Her cookbook, *The Racing Gourmet*, with recipes themed around each NASCAR Sprint Cup Series event, was due to be launched at Daytona next year.

Grace's knowledge of all things NASCAR included having an inside track on its most famous participants, along with its most infamous. Like Brent.

"Wow." Grace slid onto the stool beside her sister's. "Exactly how involved are you?"

"Enough that it scares me." Hope gave her head a derisive shake. "He claims he was set up to take the fall in the Fuelgate scandal. He sounds totally believable."

"So did Rat-Face when he swore to you that he had nothing to do with bilking money from those widows."

"Exactly. And I believed every word he said. Up until the police showed up and hauled his butt off to jail." Hope shifted her gaze across the kitchen where a handful of Grace's employees were busy boxing up champagne flutes and serving platters. Another worker was wiping down the huge commercial ovens inset into the wall. Still another scoured the deep sinks.

"I *like* Brent," she said softly. "He's smart and has this wry wit. And he's a super pilot, so I have no problem putting my life into his hands every time we take off."

"Trusting him with your heart is an entirely different matter," Grace said.

Hope remet her sister's understanding gaze. "He could be lying to my face about his part in the scandal. Knowing that—just *knowing* it—should stop me from wanting to rip his clothes off and jump his bones. It doesn't."

"Well." Grace blew out a breath. "Sounds serious."

The thought that it could be put fluttering wings of panic in Hope's belly. "I told him I need to take things slow. That we had to be friends first before we could be anything else. We're going to date for now, is all."

"I feel it is my duty to point out that Todd and I agreed to 'just date' at first. Then our hormones got the best of us. We did try to resist each other, though."

"How long were you able to keep your hands off of each other?"

Grace's mouth curved into a wistful smile as she ran a fingertip across the gold band on her left hand. "About fifteen minutes. Hopefully you'll have more luck resisting Brent."

"Yeah," Hope said. Then she thought about the kisses they'd shared and felt her toes tingle and her blood heat. "Maybe."

"YOU GREW UP WANTING TO BE a race car driver like your dad," Hope said into the microphone of her headset as the nose of the Cessna rose into the soft autumn sky.

She and Brent had just dropped off two businessmen who had chartered a flight from Charlotte to a town in West Virginia. The plane was now headed to Dover, Delaware, where Hope planned to observe Sanford Racing's team during tomorrow's NASCAR Sprint Cup Series race. "How come you learned to fly?"

Brent adjusted a knob on the dash, then spared her a glance. The movement had rays of the late afternoon sun shooting light off the lenses of his dark glasses. "Trey."

"Trey? Was that another type of competition between you two?"

"No. It was all about secrecy." Brent tweaked a control on the GPS display's LCD screen that tracked their current location. "When Trey was a teenager, he suffered a head injury. That's when the doctors discovered he had a mild form of epilepsy. Dad didn't want that news to get out and ruin Trey's chances for a career as a driver."

"But the way Adam described Trey's condition, it sounded like he's never had a seizure." A tricky patch of crosscurrents sent the plane rocking. Hope gripped the hand rest in the door. "Just rare moments that seem like he's daydreaming," she added when her heartbeat resettled.

"That's true, which is why NASCAR allows Trey to compete in races. But right after Trey's diagnosis, Dad found a reputable doctor in Mexico who specialized in treating epileptics. He bought me flying lessons so I could fly Trey to Mexico on the QT."

Wild Bobby Sanford did a lot of things on the QT, Hope thought cynically, remembering Ethan's explanation that the man had suffered a heart attack while deep-sea fishing with his mistress.

"Did you resent having to take flying lessons so you could chauffeur your baby brother around?"

"Nope. I liked piloting a plane almost as much as racing a stock car." Brent's shoulders lifted beneath his gunmetal-gray sweater. "Since flying is how I make my living now, Dad's insistence on secrecy turned out to be a benefit for me."

"A huge one."

Suddenly cold, Hope slid on her black leather jacket. After getting resettled, she checked the backup navigation map she was now nearly expert at reading, then looked out through the windscreen. They were cruising low enough that she could make out cars along the highway, towns that were little huddles of buildings and houses, and the deep, thick green of wooded areas that looked like civilization had never touched them.

"So, how's the team building going with Adam's crew?"

"We're making progress," she said, then frowned at the thought of Luis Macha's reaction to Brent's presence at the race track two weeks ago. She was still puzzling over that, but for various reasons she had no intention of discussing it with Brent. "Adam's working hard at getting his team back on track."

"Thanks to you."

Hope sent him a sassy look. "All in a day's work. Or in this case, a few weeks."

"Speaking of weeks, how much longer do you expect to work for Sanford Racing?"

"I should be able to leave things in Adam's hands by early next month." She attributed the sudden hollowness in her stomach to another spot of turbulence. For the first time, the prospect of returning home to Dallas after she wrapped up a job didn't hold a lot of appeal.

She didn't have to wonder why. There wouldn't exactly be a lot of chance for her and Brent's *friendship with benefits* to develop.

As if reading her mind, he said, "Next month isn't far off." He'd taken his shades off in deference to the darkening sky. His eyes, in the whitish glow of the dash lights, were a rich, warm chocolate-brown.

"I know." She reached for one of the granola-and-fruit bars she'd tucked into her jacket's pocket. "Guess we're going to have to figure out how to date from a distance."

"We're going to have to figure out a lot—"

A violent bump sent the granola bar flying and had Hope grabbing for a handhold. "What was that?"

Narrow-eyed, Brent studied gauges while he fought to bring the nose of the plane back up. "I don't know."

"*You don't know?* What do you mean, you don't know? You're the pilot. Aren't you supposed to know?"

"Hush!" He dragged his headset off one ear, then angled his head to listen to the engine. "We're losing pressure," he said with icy calm.

The bottom dropped out of Hope's stomach as if she were on a roller-coaster ride. Her heart hammered in her chest. "What now?"

"I'm going to have to set her down."

She swallowed hard, and tasted the metallic flavor of fear. Leaning toward her window, she stared down. The sun was dipping toward the horizon, and shadows were growing with cancerous speed over the thickly wooded areas. Frantically, she searched for a clearing. "Where?"

"Check the GPS," Brent said, nodding at the screen in the dash. "See the lake with a clearing on one side of it a few degrees west?"

"Yes." Hope's lungs were working so hard, she was afraid she might hyperventilate.

Brent adjusted course, fighting the wheel as he jiggled switches. "Tell me when you see the lake," he ordered, then repositioned his headset and flipped on the radio.

While he gave a controller their plane designation and current location, Hope strained to see out into the darkening gloom. Moments later, she pointed an unsteady finger toward the horizon.

"I see the lake!" The good news was the words came out evenly, as if she wasn't on the downside of a major panic attack. The bad news was the lake appeared to be an inhospitable black blot, and the clearing on one side of it looked about as wide as a toothpick.

Brent nodded, and continued to inform the tower of their situation.

"Are you sure there's enough room for us to land?"

"We're going to find out." His voice was as grim as the look on his face.

"Oh, God."

"Doc, I need you to tighten your seat belt and hang on. This landing is going to be a little rough."

Absolute terror and helplessness gripped Hope. There was nothing she could do to help, nothing she could do to change the outcome.

Bracing her body against the seat, she held her breath as the land rushed up to meet them.

CHAPTER NINE

JAW CLENCHED, BRENT CUT the Cessna's speed, adjusting for the drag of wind as he finessed the plane toward the narrow clearance. The sky was getting darker by the minute. The shadows thickening. Setting down would be the equivalent of a night landing, which always gave the sensation that the plane was a little higher than it actually was. So, he knew to expect the gear to touch down sooner than it seemed it would.

That, however, wasn't his major concern.

What had his gut twisted in knots was the "soft-field" landing he was about to make. He had to keep the nosewheel off the ground for as long as possible before letting it touch down. Otherwise, the wheel could dig into the dirt and flip the plane over on its back.

Not good, he thought grimly. And with Hope's fear palpable in the air, there was no way he was going to share any of those details with her.

"You holding on, Doc?" Even though he had enough adrenaline pumping through him to light up a city, he forced his voice to remain even.

"If I was holding on any tighter, I'd rip off a chunk of this armrest." Coming through his headset, her voice sounded thick with dread.

Brent knew the feeling. Trying to put a plane down

on a spit of land that he could barely see wasn't exactly a walk in the park on a balmy spring day.

Still, he had no choice but to deal with what faced him.

"Here we go."

THE LAST THING HOPE SAW BEFORE she squeezed her eyes shut were Brent's white-knuckled fingers locked on the controls. At the first vicious thud of wheels on land, she sucked in a breath. Held it while the plane bounced, teetered, shook, then rolled to a halt.

"Are you okay, Doc?" he asked instantly.

"I...think so." Opening her eyes, she forced the trapped air out of her lungs. Her stomach was churning, but apart from that she was in one piece. Thank God. "Yes, I'm fine. How about you?"

"I'll know in a minute." Brent reached out, grabbed her face in both of his hands and dragged her, straining against her seat belt, close enough to kiss. "Yeah, I'm one hundred percent," he said, and kissed her again. "No doubt about it."

Jerking back, she gaped at him. The man was actually *smiling*.

With emotion storming through her like gale winds, she wasn't sure what to do—laugh or scream. Maybe both. "What the heck do you think you're doing?"

"Taking advantage of my 'friends with benefits' status. If we were simply friends, I'd have shaken your hand over the fact we made it down alive."

"Alive." She didn't relax, exactly, but the alarm pumping inside of her began to wane at that reminder. "Okay, good point. Alive *is* reason for celebration." Her hands were still shaking so badly that she balled them into fists. "Look, I wouldn't mind getting out of this plane so I could feel some ground under my feet."

"Not a problem." Brent radioed an update to the controller, then pulled off his headset and unbuckled his seat belt. "Just give me a minute to grab a flashlight and check out our surroundings. See if there's any wildlife we startled."

"Wildlife?" she asked, even as he opened his door and climbed out.

Hope punched the release button on her seat belt, then leaned forward, peering uneasily through the gloom. Which was mostly wasted effort, since all she could make out were silhouettes of treetops against the murky sky.

Then she saw the beam of Brent's flashlight stab into the darkness. It was incredibly bright, racing across the expanse of trees which threw huge shadows behind them that in her reeling imagination seemed to move.

A tingle of unease touched the back of her neck like a cool wind. "Great," she muttered as she returned her headset to its hook.

Moments later, Brent came around the plane, opened her door and helped her out. She took a deep gulp of fresh, crisp air and tried out her legs. Not too unsteady, she discovered, pleased.

She swept her gaze across the trees, hoping to spot a light from a nearby cabin. All she saw was darkness. "Exactly where are we?"

"Far enough from civilization that we won't be able to fly out until tomorrow."

"Fly out? Did you say *fly out?*"

"I did."

"I'm not sure I want to fly again. Ever."

With the lights of the plane's interior on, there was

no missing the appraising look he gave her. "I feel it my duty to point out that we didn't crash. We simply had to divert here due to engine trouble."

"But there's no runway." She flapped a hand toward the distant trees. "No...*nothing*. Don't we need like, a tow truck?"

"We won't know what we need until morning when there's enough light for me to pull out my toolbox and have a look at the engine. Until then, we stay put."

"The morning?" Hope managed when she found her voice. "But...you were on the radio. You told the controller where we are. Isn't he sending some sort of rescue team in?"

"This place is so remote, it would take hours for anyone to drive in here. By that time, it'd be nearly dawn. And, remember from looking at the map how little land there is between the trees and the lake? Bottom line is, there isn't room to land another plane safely."

"Ever heard of a helicopter? One could set down and lift us out."

"Probably, but it would be risky for the pilot to try to land in such a small area when it's pitch-black out." He reached out and squeezed her upper arm. "Doc, we're not injured. The plane's undamaged physically. I've got a hunch that the problem is with the carburetor. That's why I told the controller I'd see if I could do the repairs on-site and keep in contact. He'll notify my office manager. Mo'll let both of our families know what's going on. I don't think our cell phones will work out here." His hand slid down the sleeve of her leather jacket, his fingers skimming her wrist. "With a few minor adjustments I'll probably be able to fly us out in the morning."

Her head was hammering. Why did the man have to sound so logical, so perfectly and completely right in the assessment of their situation? Not to mention calm and totally in charge.

Focus, she told herself. There was nothing she could do to change their situation. So, she simply had to deal with it.

Easing out a resigned breath, she looked at the plane. "At least tell me the seats recline so we don't have to sleep sitting up."

"Actually, since we're in the four-seater Skylane, there's a better place than the seats to get comfortable in."

With the air getting colder, she slid her hands into the pockets of her wool slacks. "Where?"

Aiming the flashlight's beam, he walked to the rear of the plane, pulled open a good-sized hatch. "The baggage compartment has room enough for both of us to stretch out."

Hope watched as he set the flashlight on the floor of the compartment, then began shifting items.

"We'll move your suitcase and my duffel into the backseat," he said over his shoulder. "I always carry a couple of blankets and we've got bottled water." He straightened, then grinned at her. "Good thing there's plenty of Sanford Aviation's complimentary peanuts, so we won't starve."

"Wonderful," Hope muttered, wishing they had a box of her sister's hors d'oeuvres. "I've got a couple of granola bars in my bag. And a few breath mints."

"That's the spirit."

Just then, thunder rumbled through the dark sky. Brent glanced up. "We'd better climb inside and make ourselves comfortable for the night."

"NO BARS." RESIGNED, HOPE turned off her cell phone. Sitting on the floor of the luggage compartment, facing the rear of the plane, she tried to settle her shoulders more comfortably against the padded interior.

Crouched beside her, Brent pulled the hatch closed, secured it, then opened a storage bin. "It was worth a try to see if you could make a call."

"Hmm…" Now that he was inside with her, Hope did a narrow-eyed study of the compartment. He was right, it would shelter both of them—as long as they reclined thigh-to-thigh.

The nerves that had begun to settle after their emergency landing began to twist, tight and hot beneath her skin. This was the man who'd kissed her senseless. Twice. The man whom she'd resolved to take time getting to know. The man she had no idea if she could trust.

Now, here they were, basically joined at the hip and shacked up for the night in the middle of nowhere.

Instantly, suspicion grew in her brain like a shadow at dusk. "Sanford, tell me this isn't your version of the 'my car ran out of gas, we'll have to spend the night stranded together in the boonies' routine."

BRENT'S HANDS FISTED on the blankets he'd tugged out of the bin. If he had been with any other woman but Hope, he'd have laughed at the remark. Finessed it into a way to get close and start peeling off various items of clothing.

But the eyes of the woman sitting across from him were filled with wariness and nerves. That was all the reminder he needed that Hope Hunt trusted him about as much as she trusted her own ability to fly the Cessna.

Which made total sense, considering her background with the lying con man she'd planned to marry.

"Have you ever camped out?" he asked, handing her one of the blankets. Rain started to patter on the plane's roof, like fingers lightly drumming on a table. "Just sat around, telling stories around the campfire?"

"Never." She spread the blanket from her waist to the tips of her black leather ankle boots. "I'm a city girl. I'll take room service any day to roughing it."

He pulled a small battery-powered lantern out of the bin, turned it on, then snapped off the flashlight. "Well, since we're here, how about we pretend this lantern is our campfire."

"Works for me." She pursed her mouth. "Does that mean you're going to tell me a sit-around-the-campfire story?"

"That's the plan." He settled beside her, angling his body enough so he could see her profile. In the lantern's dim glow, her skin looked as soft as silk. He knew from experience that's exactly how it felt.

"But most campfire stories are tall tales. Mine is the truth."

"Just as long as it isn't about some harrowing almost-crash you had in one of your planes." She shoved a hand through her hair, the dark stands fanning out across her shoulders. It was not the first time he'd imagined it spread across his pillow. His chest. His thighs. "We do still have to fly out of here tomorrow morning," she added.

"Yeah." He eased out a breath, reshifted his thoughts. "I want to tell you about what happened to me at Talladega," he said quietly.

Emotion flickered in her gray eyes. "Are you sure you want to talk about it?"

"Truth is, Doc, it's the last thing I want to talk about."
He pulled open a nearby storage bin, handed her a bottle
of water, retrieved one for himself. "But what happened
then is the reason you don't trust me. Maybe if you hear
the truth about Fuelgate, you someday will. Otherwise,
I figure I'll be stuck forever as one of your 'friends
with benefits.'" He looked at her steadily as he slid his
fingertips across the back of her hand that rested against
her thigh. "That's not what I want, Hope. I want more."

HOPE'S SKIN TINGLED AND HER heartbeat thickened in
response to his touch. She knew that single moments,
both simple and dramatic, could alter courses forever.
A deep, intuitive awareness told her this was one of
those times.

Her mouth dry, she unscrewed the bottle's cap,
took a long, slow drink of the tepid water. "Tell me
what happened."

"Just before the race started, Alan Cargill showed up
in our garage area and took Adam aside." Brent paused.
"Your dad was crew chief for Cargill Motors then,
right?"

"Yes," she replied simply. She saw no need to
mention that her father had taken the entire Fuelgate
incident personally.

"Adam brought Cargill over to talk to me. The man
was livid, saying that his driver, Kent Grosso, had just
been disqualified from the race because his fuel was
contaminated. I said that was a shame, but I didn't know
why Cargill was telling me.

"Cargill said they'd been sabotaged by their gas man,
Mike Jones. That Jones had come to him immediately,
suffering from a pang of conscience, and confessed that

I had bribed him to do it." He dragged a hand through his hair. "Needless to say, I was shocked. I told Cargill I didn't know what the hell he was talking about and that the accusation was a lie."

Her gaze followed Brent's over the top of the backseats to the window where raindrops ran like tears. The silence stretched while he stared into the darkness.

"Adam backed me up," he said finally. "But as team owner, he had no choice but to withdraw me from the race. If he didn't, NASCAR would, and it was better to do it voluntarily. I knew he had no choice, but I was mad as hell. I'd taken the pole for that race. I was headed for Victory Lane, and suddenly my world had turned upside down."

The splinter of old pain that had worked its way into his voice tightened Hope's chest.

"I told Cargill there was no way he had any proof that I'd had anything to do with the sabotage. That's when things got really bad. Cargill told me Jones swore that a member of the Sanford Racing team had called him and asked him to meet me at the Speedway Bar."

"A member of the Sanford Racing team was involved in the sabotage?" Hope asked instantly, her thoughts darting to Luis Macha, the front tire carrier.

Brent's mouth went tight. "I wouldn't know, since I wasn't involved. Which is what I'm trying to tell you."

She closed her eyes. "I'm sorry. What you said had my mind jumping to something going on now with Adam's pit crew."

"Something that might go back four years?"

"I don't know." She mentally filed away the information for later. "So, you supposedly met Mike Jones at the Speedway Bar. Had you been there before?"

"Off and on over the years, but I'd certainly never

arranged to meet Cargill's gas man there, or anywhere for that matter. I didn't even know who the hell the guy was, and I told Cargill that."

"What did he say?"

"Nothing. All of a sudden he produced a surveillance tape from the bar that showed me talking to Jones. When I saw the tape, it stirred a memory of a vague encounter I'd had there with him. I was standing at the bar, waiting for the beer I'd ordered. Jones walked up, asked me a question about the upcoming race. I answered him. Then I picked up my beer and walked off, out of range of the camera. That's when Jones started giving the camera surreptitious looks and swivelling his head like he was trying to see if anyone was watching him. Then he wandered off camera in the same direction I went. That made it look like we were having some sort of clandestine meeting, supposedly where money changed hands."

"How much money?"

"Jones claimed I paid him five hundred dollars cash up-front to add some supposedly untraceable compound into the fuel tank of Kent Grosso's car before the race. And that I promised to pay Jones ten grand more after Grosso's car broke down because of the tainted fuel."

"Was there a record of any money changing hands?"

"The evidence Jones offered was a deposit slip dated the day after we were both at the bar. It showed five hundred dollars had been deposited into his checking account."

Hope studied Brent's face while rain pelted the roof of the plane. His expression was impenetrable. Yet, there was something tugging on her heart, telling her to believe him.

But memories of how her ex had been just as convincing had her stiffening her spine and shifting into analytical psychologist mode. "Why would this Mike Jones go to all the trouble to sabotage his own team's car if it wasn't true?"

"That was an answer I wanted myself," Brent replied. "So, I confronted Jones right after seeing the video. We argued. My temper got away from me and I slugged him. Right before bystanders pulled us apart, the bastard got this ugly look on his face and whispered, 'I did it for *her.*'"

Hope blinked. "Her, who?"

"I have no idea. When I went looking for Jones the next day to find out, he was gone. Packed all of his belongings and disappeared. I've looked for him over the years. Hired a private detective to try to find him. The guy might as well have never existed."

"You still have no idea who the woman was?"

"No clue. I've racked my brain trying to figure out if a woman in my past had reason to get back at me for some unknown grievance. I've come up empty."

Hope trailed her gaze over his clear-cut profile, the hard geometry of his jaw, the no-nonsense curve of his mouth. Professionally she'd been lied to by patients and had become adept at spotting dishonesty. Personally, she'd proven that when emotions got tossed into the mix, her objectivity went out the window. She'd taken her fiancé's word at face value. She wasn't willing to do the same with Brent.

"Why didn't you try to defend yourself against Jones's accusations?"

"I considered that. But with no solid proof that Jones was the one who was lying, I always seemed to come across as the one making excuses, denying things. No one questioned how quickly the surveillance video showed up. NASCAR suspended me from racing, pending their investigation into the matter, so the season was lost for me. A legal battle would have gone on for months, maybe years, and there was no guarantee that I could clear my name. That would have dragged down Sanford Racing. So, I walked away. Moved on. I've built my own business from the ground up and, for the most part, I'm satisfied with the way things are."

Hope saw a look cross his face. "What is it?"

"Just thinking about how a possible chance to clear myself died with Alan Cargill."

"What do you mean?"

"At the latest NASCAR awards banquet, he told Adam he'd stumbled on to something that made him think maybe Jones had set me up after all."

"Did he tell Adam what he'd found out?"

"No, Cargill wanted to talk to both Adam and myself the following day. Unfortunately, he was murdered that night."

Hope put a hand to her throat. "I wonder what Uncle Alan found out."

Brent arched a brow. "*Uncle* Alan?"

"Our families weren't officially related, but my dad worked for Cargill Racing for years. He and Uncle Alan were best friends."

"Then I guess you've heard all the sordid details about me."

"Some."

"Enough." Brent took her hand in his. "I didn't think it mattered what anyone else thought about me because I knew I hadn't stepped over the line. But then you climbed into my plane and now it matters to me what you think." His fingers linked with hers. "I didn't cheat at Talladega. I didn't *need* to cheat. I would have won that race. I told the truth then, and I'm telling it now. If I could hand you the proof it would take for you to believe me, I would."

Hope looked into his eyes. There was tightness in her chest again, but not the sort that presaged nerves. Or wariness. It was the flexing, she thought, of something starting to open again.

And suddenly, she knew what lay beneath the surface of this man. In addition to the intensely sensual threat he posed, there was strength and honor and integrity. *Dear, God, am I falling in love with him?*

She lifted a hand to touch his cheek. "I believe you," she said quietly. "Totally."

"Why?"

"I'm not sure. Instinct. Intuition. Sixth sense, maybe." She looked down at the hand linked with hers. "All the times my fiancé swore to me that he hadn't bilked rich old ladies out of their money, I wanted to believe him. I loved him, and I wanted to believe. It wasn't until after he was arrested that I realized every time he swore to me that he was innocent, I felt on edge, like I was missing something that was right in front of me. But something inside of me wouldn't let me look too hard at his explanations." She shook her head. "With you, there's nothing niggling at me, no little twinge at the base of my spine telling me your story doesn't add up. You're telling the truth. I know it."

When Brent shifted toward her, she saw the raw emotion in his eyes. "I give you my word, Hope. I won't lie to you. Ever."

"I told you I believe you."

"So you did."

He lifted their joined hands, brushed his lips over her knuckles. "But that's not all I want from you."

The deepening of his voice, his words delivered an instantaneous punch to her belly. "I've got a good idea what that is," she murmured.

His wicked, way sexy smile had her fighting her own smile. "Do you think I'm about to try to renegotiate just what all our 'friends with benefits' agreement involves?"

"That crossed my mind." And, dammit, she was tempted to let the desire churning inside of her over-power logic.

"Mine, too." In the dim light from the lantern, she watched his expression turn serious. In a finger-snap of time, all levity vanished, replaced by a tension as old as Adam and Eve.

"I want you, Hope. Want to peel that leather jacket off of you, along with the rest of your clothes, and spend this long, rainy night making love with you. But that won't get me all that I want."

"There's more?" she asked, the rawness of her emotions unraveling in her voice.

"Trust." He cupped her face in his hands. "I want you to trust me. To be sure of me. I don't want you to ever wonder again if I'm like that slime who broke your heart." He leaned forward, brushed his mouth over hers. "Whatever else this turns out to be, it isn't about being just friends."

His mouth moved to hers, brushing, nipping, then taking, in a dreamy kind of possession that had her own vision blurring.

The humming in her brain increased until it was a

wall of sound, unrecognizable. She could feel the little flames start to flare beneath every pulse point in her body, then spread long, patient fingers of fire outward. Everywhere.

When he raised his head slowly, breaking off the kiss, she nearly moaned in frustration.

His fingertips stroked her cheek. The quiet touch was somehow wildly passionate, desperately intimate.

"Definitely not just friends," he murmured.

CHAPTER TEN

THE RAIN MOVED ON BEFORE DAWN. With the morning sky filled with sparkling sunshine, Hope spread a blanket on the ground outside the plane while Brent worked on the faulty carburetor.

Wishing she had a cup of steaming coffee to go along with her granola bar, she pulled her laptop out of her briefcase.

While the cool whisper of a breeze ruffled her hair, she typed the facts Brent had related about the Fuelgate scandal. Along the way, she made notes on ideas of how to deal with several issues regarding Adam's crew members.

One being Sanford Racing's front tire carrier, Luis Macha. If he believed Mike Jones's story about one of the pit crew members aiding Brent in the alleged sabotage, it stood to reason there could be a measure of distrust and suspicion among all of the team members who'd worked there four years ago. Those unresolved feelings could have added to the lack of cohesion among the personnel. And perhaps had something to do with the bad pit stop two weeks ago in Richmond. She was anxious to get to the track in Dover and talk to Luis.

That, however, wouldn't happen unless Brent figured out how to repair the plane.

Her gaze drifted to him. He stood on the short set of wooden steps he'd retrieved from somewhere inside the plane while he worked on the engine. A small toolbox sat open on the ground; a rag stuck out of the back pocket of his slacks. She smiled to herself when he found several interesting names to call a bolt he fought to loosen.

His dark hair was rumpled, the sleeves of his gunmetal-gray sweater shoved up on his forearms. His dark sunglasses, combined with the stubble covering his jaw, only made him look that much more delectable. Desirable. As if he'd just climbed out of bed.

Which, basically he had.

Hope sighed as her thoughts went back to the dark, rainy hours she'd spent snuggled in his arms. Both of them fully clothed. And in the hover of time between consciousness and sleep, she had felt herself sliding contentedly into love.

Dear Lord, she was in love, she thought helplessly. In love with a man who'd spent the past four years scorned by his peers, coworkers and friends who had thought the worst about him. Even his baby brother believed he wasn't above cheating and lying.

But he'd done neither, she was sure of that. Some-how, someway, she was going to figure out how to help Brent clear his name. Jaw firmed with decision, she turned her attention back to her notes.

She was still typing ideas when the sound of the plane's engine springing to life brought her chin up.

"We're good to go," Brent shouted, then shut off the engine.

"We can take off now?"

"As soon as I clean up." He checked his watch, then climbed out of the pilot's seat, holding a bottle of water and a rag. "If everything goes smoothly, you should be at the track a couple of hours before the race starts."

Hope rose and began folding the blanket. "I know the original plan was for you to pick up a charter in Dover when you dropped me off there yesterday. And I was to fly back to Charlotte on the team's plane."

"Mo would have made other arrangements for my charter when the controller called to let her know we had to set down here for the night." He pulled a can of degreaser from the toolbox and went to work on his hands. "When we get into the air, I'll radio the FBO at the Dover airport and arrange for a thorough check of the Skylane's engine. That'll take most of the day. If you want to fly back to Charlotte with me instead of the team's plane, I'll wait for you."

Glancing up from his hands, he sent her a slow, lazy smile. "Or you could just stay here all day with me and forego the race."

Hope thrilled to the clutch of lust deep in her center. "As tempting as that sounds, I don't think playing hooky would do much for my professional reputation."

"Or your personal one," he added while scrubbing the rag over his knuckles.

She draped the folded blanket over one forearm, then picked up her briefcase. "I don't view hanging around with you as something that will put a black mark on my name."

"You'd better think again, Doc. Because of Fuelgate, I'm persona non grata to most people involved with NASCAR. Which includes just about your entire family."

"When they learn the truth about Fuelgate, that will change."

"Maybe in your rainbow world," he said quietly while he returned the degreaser to the toolbox, then shut its lid. "In my darker version, the way people view me won't change unless I find rock-solid proof that I was set up. I've been trying to do that for four years."

Hope angled her chin like a sword. She had dedicated her life to helping people.

Whatever it took, she was going to figure out some way to help the man she loved.

A FEW HOURS LATER, HOPE WALKED into the catering area at the track in Dover. The area consisted of a motor home with a canvas awning pulled out on one side, food displayed buffet-style beneath. Several car manufacturers had provided the meal today for all the teams, something Hope was grateful for since granola bars and peanuts had been all she'd eaten during the past twenty-four hours.

She glanced around. The air smelled of hot dogs and barbecue, the familiar odor reminding her of the races she'd attended with her father while growing up.

Her stomach growled a demand for nourishment.

Despite that, eating wasn't her first priority. Talking to Luis Macha was.

She spotted him at the buffet, filling a plate. He was dressed in Sanford Racing's blue and yellow colors, as was Griff Fletcher, the team's front tire changer, already seated at a table in the covered eating area.

Hope hung back, watching as Luis balanced a roll on top of his food, grabbed a soft drink, then headed for a table on the opposite side of the eating area where Fletcher sat. She retrieved a plate, spooned up some shredded barbecue beef and a scoop of potato salad, then headed for the table where Luis was the only occupant.

"Hi, Luis, mind if I join you?"

The front tire carrier glanced up from his plate, his dark eyes looking as tense as always. "Free country."

Hope slid onto the chair opposite his, figuring he would have rather gone swimming with sharks than dine with her.

She sent him a cheery smile. "A snag came up in my travel plans, so I just now got here." She had, however, taken time to change into a fresh sweater and slacks, and anchored her hair back with a tortoiseshell headband, so at least she didn't look as if she'd spent the night in the wilderness. "How did Trey do during qualifying?"

"Ninth."

"Not bad." Hope speared a piece of beef. It was warm and tangy and tasted like heaven. So did the second bite.

"Luis, remember last week when you told me you don't like being associated with anything to do with cheating? And because of that, you quit working for Sanford Racing after the Fuelgate scandal?"

His eyes went wary as he bit into a piece of chicken. "Yeah."

"Is the cheating issue why you're not sitting over there with Griff Fletcher?"

"Don't know what you mean."

"You and Griff work closer together than almost any other team members. Neither one of you can do your job without the other."

He swabbed a paper napkin across his chin. "So?"

Hope took a bite of potato salad. She didn't know if her theory would hold water, but there was no time like the present to find out. "So, your work can't help but suffer if you suspect your closest colleague of playing a part in the Fuelgate scandal."

Astonishment crossed Luis's face. Replaced by uneasiness. He stabbed his fork into a mound of coleslaw. "I never said that."

"No, you didn't. What you said was that you didn't like it when Brent Sanford showed up at the Richmond track. Seeing him probably reminded you that you suspected Fletcher was the team member who was supposed to have called Cargill Motors' gas man and set up his meeting with Brent Sanford at the Speedway Bar. That's when Brent purportedly paid Mike Jones to contaminate the fuel in Kent Grosso's car."

Hunching his broad shoulders, Luis sent a narrow-eyed look at his coworker. "Griff hangs out at the Speedway Bar. It's no secret he has a girlfriend who likes the finer things in life, so he's always looking for ways to earn extra cash. If Sanford offered him money to set up the meet between him and Mike Jones, Griff would have made the call."

Relieved that her theory had scored a bull's-eye and that Luis was finally opening up, Hope forked up another bite of potato salad. "I'm going to tell you something, and I'm asking you to take what I say on faith. I don't have any proof that it's the truth. But I swear to you, it is."

His dark eyes held hers like a bug on a pin. "What?"

"Griff Fletcher didn't make that phone call. There wasn't ever any call made."

"Mike Jones swore there was. He turned himself in for contaminating Grosso's fuel."

"True. Jones did that because he has a grudge against

Brent Sanford. At this point, it appears that no one except Jones knows what it's about."

Because two crew members from another team had settled at the end of their table, Hope leaned in and lowered her voice so she wouldn't be overheard. "It's understandable why you thought Griff was the one who made the phone call. In your place, I'd have thought the same thing. But it just didn't happen."

Luis regarded her for a long moment. "Say you're right. What changes if there isn't any proof?"

"If you take what I say on faith, everything changes." It had for her when she'd accepted Brent's word as the truth. "So, maybe now when you work with Griff, you won't have to be thinking about anything else but getting the job done."

"I don't know." Luis slid another look his coworker's way. "Faith is one thing. It'd be a lot better if you had solid proof."

"I PREFER THIS TYPE OF LANDING to the one we made last night," Brent commented after he set the Cessna down at the Charlotte airport.

"I'll drink to that."

Hope removed her headset while the plane taxied to the tie-down area near the general aviation terminal. Although she'd dozed during the flight from Dover, she still felt punchy with fatigue. Thank goodness she'd be spending tonight in a bed instead of the rear of the Cessna!

She and Brent climbed out onto the tarmac while the engines on a commercial airliner thundered overhead as the big plane shoved its way into the starry night sky.

"Sanford Racing's plane beat us back," Brent said,

inclining his head toward the large jet parked nearby. The plane's steps were lowered, its interior lights on.

Hope shifted her gaze past the chain-link fence to the parking lot illuminated by the glow of security lights. She spotted Brent's black sports car in its reserved spot near the private terminal building. And recognized several Sanford Racing employees making their way toward their own cars, including Luis Macha and Griff Fletcher. She noted that Luis kept his distance from Griff. Apparently, Luis wasn't willing to take on faith that his coworker hadn't been involved in Fuelgate.

Resigned to that, Hope repositioned her purse strap over her shoulder while Brent opened the hatch to the baggage compartment. "No offense," she said, "but it's a relief just knowing I'll be staying on the ground for a while."

"None taken." He pulled out her briefcase and suitcase, then his own bag. "Before we leave here, I need to run inside to my office and pick up paperwork Mo left. How about we dump the bags in my car first?"

"Okay." Hope stifled a yawn. "But I don't need to go inside with you. I'll just wait in your car."

His low chuckle had her sliding him a sideways look as they walked toward the gate in the chain-link fence. "What?"

"Something tells me when I get back to the car, I'll find you napping like you did during most of the return flight."

"A crack navigator never naps on duty." She tossed her hair back. "I was merely resting my eyes."

"Yeah, right." He checked his watch. "Good thing I don't need to get my land legs back before I take off again."

"How soon is that?"

"First thing in the morning, I've got a charter to Alaska. Every year I fly a couple of CEOs there to hunt."

Hope furrowed her forehead as they stepped through the gate. The thought of him leaving town had tightened her throat. Which was ridiculous. The man was a pilot—he made his living flying people wherever they wanted to go. Just because she had fallen in love with him was no reason for her to start getting clingy.

Thinking about how much had changed in the past twenty-four hours was enough to make her head spin. She was going to have to figure out how to deal with her overwhelming feelings for a man she'd known for such a short time.

"When will you be back?" she asked when they reached his car.

He aimed the remote; the snick of the doors and trunk unlocking sounded on the night air. "I won't know until I check the paperwork on upcoming charters Mo left on my desk. At the latest, I'll be back in time to fly you to the race next weekend."

While he loaded the trunk, Hope glanced back toward Sanford Racing's plane in time to see Trey Sanford striding down the plane's steps. He had the strap of a duffel slung over one shoulder and his cell phone clamped to his ear. "There's Trey. I imagine he's still fired up from finishing third today."

Brent shut the trunk's lid and glanced in his brother's direction. "No doubt."

Going with impulse, she said, "You should talk to him."

"About placing third? Already done. I called his cell when I heard the race results. Told him he did a super job."

"I mean, talk to him about Fuelgate. Tell him what you told me."

"Adam gave him my side of the story." Brent's voice had hardened around the edges. "Trey chose not to believe it."

"That's not the same as hearing it from you." Noting the annoyance that had settled in Brent's face, she softened her voice. "Have you ever tried to talk to Trey?"

Gazing down at her, he crossed his arms over his chest. "Am I talking to Dr. Hunt now? You trying to *shrink* me?"

"Hardly. I just don't want you to regret something you can maybe fix with a little conversation." She heard the echo of sadness in her own voice. If only her mother had talked to her about the secret burden Hope was sure she'd carried. For the rest of her life, she would wonder if she could have spared her mother a measure of pain if she'd just pushed her a little harder to open up.

She didn't want Brent to have that same kind of regret over his brother.

"You can't rubber stamp what's between me and Trey." In the glow of the security lights, Brent's eyes looked as hard as copper. "It isn't something that can be fixed by sitting down and having a chat. That's because he needs proof Mike Jones set me up."

"You didn't need proof to convince me," she pointed out gently. "I took your word for it."

"I know, Doc." Brent eased closer, his body heat wrapping around her as he skimmed a finger down her cheek. "And that makes me a very happy man."

Frustration mixed with fatigue made her head pound. "If you would at least try to talk to Trey, he might do the same."

"And he might not." Brent's mouth dipped toward hers as he murmured, "My brother is not what I care about right now."

That compelling mouth so close to her own put a kick of lust in her belly. She looked into his eyes. "Life isn't like racing. You don't just start in one spot, then finish in another, as fast as you can. There are curves, detours and roadblocks that have to be dealt with."

One hand curled around her nape, his thumb brushing the side of her throat. "You think I don't know that?"

"I think you believe you've grappled with everything the scandal tossed your way, handled it, and moved on. But you can't truly do that and be happy until you face what's between you and Trey."

"I've got a better idea of what will make me happy."

The low huskiness that had settled in his voice and intent glinting in his dark eyes had her annoyance needle zinging toward the top of the meter.

"Don't try to seduce me into shutting up. I get it." She pressed her palm against his chest to prevent him from leaning closer. "You don't want to talk about Trey."

He eased back. "Now we're making progress. And just to prove I don't think all talk is totally wasted, you and I can chat on the drive to your dad's house."

"About how hardheaded you are?" she asked through gritted teeth.

"Actually, I was thinking more along the lines of how we're going to work this dating-from-a-distance business when you go back to Dallas for good."

Fighting her frustration, Hope let it go. "All right."

The grin he flashed her was bold, reckless and irresistible. "I'll be back in a few minutes. Try to grab some more shut-eye while I'm gone."

Scowling, she watched him swipe an ID card on the reader beside the terminal door, then disappear inside. It hurt her heart to think he might never mend the rift with his brother, but she couldn't force him to talk to Trey.

She had just pulled open the passenger door and tossed her purse inside when she heard footsteps approach.

"Well, well."

Hope turned at the sound of Trey's voice. Took a deep breath to try to ease her frustration. "Hello, Trey."

"Hello yourself." He gave her the identical cocky grin as his brother. "From what I just saw, that clinch I caught you and Brent in at the museum was just a warm-up of things to come."

She sent him a bland smile. "Congratulations on the race today."

"Thanks." He unlocked the forest-green sports car parked nearby. "So, it seems to me the race team is working together more smoothly," he said as he stowed his duffel in the car's trunk. "Adam says that's your doing."

Considering that her talk with Luis Macha apparently hadn't resulted in his warming up to Griff Fletcher, she still had a lot of work to do.

"Adam's working hard with the team, but nothing's really been resolved. The fact that your medical condition was kept a secret for so long caused a lot of resentment."

"Yeah, I understand. We just decided it would be best to focus attention on my racing, not on my health. Do you agree?"

"Keeping the team in the dark about your condition for so long resulted in a breakdown of trust between you and Adam and the team. But that isn't the only resent-ment causing the problem."

Trey leaned against the driver's door of his car. "What do you mean?"

"Your distrust of Brent plays a part, too. Because of how your team perceives the relationship between you and your brother, it affects how they view you."

"Why should they even care about that?" His voice hardened, but he acted as though he wanted to know. "It doesn't have anything to do with them."

"Adam is their boss, but you're their leader," Hope said. "How you deal with things affects the people you work with. They all feel you didn't trust them enough to tell them about your medical condition. They see you not trusting Brent. Why should *they* trust anyone on the team? It feeds on itself."

"You really think Fuelgate has something to do with the way the team works now?" he asked flatly. "Four years later?"

"I do." She hesitated. Brent might not like her men-tioning Fuelgate, but the bottom line was, the effects from the scandal were one reason her client had hired her. And Trey was asking her opinion. She couldn't give him anything but an honest answer. "It's also spilled over into other parts of your life."

Trey kept his gaze locked with hers. "I'm listening."

"Your relationship with Brent took a hit because of the scandal. That affects not only your racing, but your family, especially your mother."

"What about my mother?"

"She told me that after the scandal, Brent didn't just walk away from racing. He pulled emotionally away from the family." Because the night air had taken on a sudden chill, Hope wrapped her arms around her waist. "You turned away from the family, too, Trey, when you chose not to believe Brent. That's a natural instinct, to pull away so it wouldn't cause more conflict in your family. Apparently you and Brent have managed to make things work between you on a superficial level. You can interact with each other and remain civil, but the people around you feel the tension. Nothing's going to improve between you unless one of you takes a step and talks to the other one about what happened."

"I never accused Brent of cheating," Trey said defensively. "I never said I believed he did. Our family presented a united front."

"Except it really didn't."

Overhead, the *whomp, whomp* of a helicopter's blades sounded. Hope glanced up and saw the chopper's lights against the night sky.

"If Brent cared what I thought, why didn't he ever ask me?"

Her gaze shifted back to Trey. "Maybe you should ask *him*." His narrowed eyes told Hope that Trey didn't like what she was saying, but at least he wasn't shutting her down the way Brent had.

"Brent learned to fly because you had to have someone trustworthy to take you to Mexico on the sly," she said quietly.

"Yeah. Our dad didn't want anyone knowing about my condition because it might mess up my chances of driving in NASCAR-sanctioned races. That's why Brent became a pilot, to keep the secret." Trey raised a hand. "What does that have to do with Fuelgate?"

"Quite simply, Brent was there for you when you needed him."

"That's enough, Hope."

Brent's hardened voice, coming from just inches behind her, made her jump—and shot her heart into her throat.

Light fingers of wind dragged at her hair as she turned. If she'd been fainter of heart, the look in his eyes would have had her taking a step back in defense.

"You planning on psychoanalyzing my entire family?"

"That's not what's going on here. Trey asked me how I thought the race team was doing."

"And my flying him to Mexico when we were teen-agers relates to that how?"

Because she had no ready answer for that, she dragged in a breath, turned to Trey. "I apologize if anything I said made you feel uncomfortable."

He gave them both a curt nod. "Time for me to head home." Trey slid into his car. Seconds later, its engine roared to life, then the car disappeared into the night.

"Brent—"

"If you're riding with me, you need to get into my car." There was a gleaming edge on every word. "Now."

She stood her ground. "Look, I'm sorry you're upset—"

"Damn right I am." His voice snapped out like a slap.

She held up a hand, palm toward him. "Trey was off on medical leave when I first came to work for Sanford Racing. Between that and his promotional schedule we haven't had a chance to meet one-on-one. So, when he walked up, he asked me how things are progressing with the racing team."

"I told you about what was going on between my brother and me in confidence. Do you betray all of your clients and patients this way?"

Twin demons of hurt and temper stabbed at her. "We both know our relationship doesn't fall under either category." Her heart quivered in her chest, but her voice remained strong. "I care about you. It's obvious when you talk about Trey how it hurts—"

"Let me tell you what hurts. Since the day I met you, I've been trying to figure out how to earn your trust. I decided the only way to do that was to slit open a vein and tell you about the worst experience in my life. You think that was easy?"

"I know it wasn't." She reached out to place a hand on his arm, then thought better of it. It would slice at her to have him evade her touch. "I believe what you told me. I trust you."

"And that's the ironic part about all of this." His eyes blazed as he stabbed a finger in her direction. "Trust is supposed to be a two-way street, lady. Turns out, you showed me tonight what a fool I've been to trust you."

He stalked to the car and shot her a look when she didn't follow. She saw the muscle in the side of his jaw clench. "Are you coming?"

She winced at the cold fury in his voice. "I think it would be best if I take a cab."

"I'm not leaving you here."

"You won't be." She reached into the car's passenger seat, retrieved her purse. "There's a taxi right over there in front of the terminal."

Whipping around, he pulled her bag and briefcase out of the trunk. He closed it with a snap, then carried her bags to the taxi. He set them down and turned to go.

"Brent?"

"Leave it alone, Hope." He stalked back to his car and roared away.

CHAPTER ELEVEN

THE NEXT MORNING BRENT WAS still stewing over how royally he'd screwed up when he told Hope about the rift between him and Trey. What seemed like a way to open a door to her emotionally by taking her into his confidence had turned into a huge mistake. One he'd spent most of the night gnawing over.

Jaw set, he unlocked the door to Sanford Aviation and flipped on the lights in the reception area. It was a rare morning when he beat Mo to the office, but since he'd slept only in patches, he'd decided to get a head start on the preparations for that morning's charter to Alaska.

At least he could look forward to getting some flight hours in the Lear. Being at the controls of his pride and joy, along with the paperwork he had to fill out beforehand, would go a long way toward keeping thoughts of Hope at bay.

He dropped his overnight bag beside his desk, then headed to the coffeemaker.

That was as long as it took for his mind to shift back to Hope.

Dammit, why couldn't she have just kept what he'd told her about Trey to herself? he fumed while he dumped coffee into a filter. He hesitated, then added another half scoop, figuring an extra jolt of caffeine would help make up for the sleep he'd lost.

Thanks to Hope.

He had what he wanted, he told himself. His business was thriving. He'd put Fuelgate in his past. The one thing he hadn't accomplished was hunting down Mike Jones and forcing the bastard to admit the truth. But at this point that wasn't likely to happen, so he didn't dwell on it.

Despite what Dr. Sunny Disposition claimed, he *had* dealt with everything life had tossed at him. Come to terms with it. *Moved on.* Why she couldn't get that through her head was beyond him.

It was just as well he'd overheard her talking to Trey last night, he decided. That had been a blatant reminder of how easily and quickly a woman could upend a man's life.

I did it for her. Because of some woman, Mike Jones had blown Brent's world apart four years ago. He could at least be glad that, except for making things between him and Trey even more strained, Hope's sticking her nose into things wouldn't have near that same effect.

He cared about her, Brent brooded, barely aware that he'd curled his hands into fists. For the first time in his life, a woman mattered. Really *mattered*. Standing there, alone with his thoughts, he could even admit that he'd been circling perilously close to the *L* word. *Love.* Hell, he'd raced cars at blistering speeds with less fear.

That, at least, was one thing he no longer had to worry about. During his carousing days, he'd had the reputation for confining his relationships to discreet, short-term affairs. Moving on had never posed a problem. Distancing himself from Hope wouldn't be a big deal.

Or would it?

While coffee streamed into the carafe, he stared down at Mo's desk. It would take little effort on his part to jot a note telling Mo to arrange for one of the backup pilots to take over flying Hope to wherever she needed to go. And, since Sanford Racing had contracted him to fly her, he could pick up the phone and call Adam to let him know about the change. Big brother could inform Hope.

But just the thought of doing those things had something ripping inside of him.

At the same time the coffeemaker hissed up a small cloud of steam, Brent heard the office door swing inward. Expecting Mo, he grabbed two mugs.

"About time you made it to work," he said, filling the mugs with the steaming brew.

"Damn, bro, do you always get up this early?"

The sound of Trey's voice had Brent jerking his head around.

His brother ambled to the front of Mo's desk, his eyes heavy, sandy-brown hair uncombed, dark stubble on his jaw. He wore a wrinkled T-shirt, faded jeans and a jacket sporting Sanford Racing's logo.

Brent handed one of the mugs across the desk. "You look like you've been dragged through hell by the ankles."

"Stayed up late to celebrate coming in third at Dover."

Brent lifted a brow. "I thought those days ended when you and Nicole got engaged."

Trey grinned. "Who do you think I was celebrating with?"

He toasted Brent with the coffee mug, then took a sip and winced. "This stuff is strong enough to cause a nosebleed."

"You're not the only one who didn't get a lot of sleep last night," Brent muttered, then took a swig of his own coffee. It had a harder kick than he'd intended, but since Trey had shown up, he had more important things to discuss.

"I'd planned on calling you before I took off."

Trey hitched a hip up on the edge of the desk. "About Hope, I imagine."

"Yeah."

"I thought about calling you, too. Decided it was best to talk face-to-face."

Resigned that he was about to have the conversation with his brother that he'd gone out of his way for four years to avoid, Brent settled in Mo's sturdy chair. "I'll start by apologizing for what Hope said. I told her some things in confidence. Didn't mean for them to get back to you."

"I admit, I didn't like hearing them."

"Don't blame you. You've got a right to your opinion about me and Fuelgate. I hope there aren't any hard feelings."

"After Nicole and I got our celebrating out of the way, I told her about my conversation with Hope." Trey stared down into his mug for a long moment. "Nicole suggested that maybe it'd be a smart move on my part to look at things from the angle Hope laid them out. Wasn't easy, but I did. And it hit me, that maybe you're the one who ought to have the hard feelings, and not just about Fuelgate."

Leaning back in his chair, Brent crossed his arms over his chest. "What else is there?"

"Let's start with the way things have always been between us." Trey set his mug on the desk. "For as long as I can remember, it seemed you got whatever you wanted, no matter what. It was like you were one of those people born with gold on the tips of their fingers. You reached for something, it was suddenly yours."

Brent furrowed his brow. "Things sure as hell didn't seem that way to me."

"Different perspectives," Trey said with a shrug. "In school I'd maybe get a B if I studied until my brains leaked out of my ears. You would ace a test without opening a book. You just absorbed stuff. But it wasn't only schoolwork that you were better at. It was every-thing. Dad was always praising how you did things, then telling me I had to work a little harder. Just work a little harder and I'd be as good as you."

Brent didn't hear full-blown resentment in his brother's voice, just a whisper of it. Still, it put a knot in his throat. "I never heard Dad say that to you. If I had, I'd have spoken up."

"Since he was all about our competing for every-thing, I doubt that would have stopped him."

"Probably not," Brent agreed.

"When I was diagnosed with epilepsy, I was barely sixteen. Mad over the fact I had this incurable disease. It didn't occur to me how lucky I was to have the support of my entire family, or how my condition affected everybody, especially you. Dad made you learn to fly so you could ferry me to Mexico."

"Hey, Dad didn't force me to take flying lessons. I wanted to learn."

"Even so, I never once gave a thought to how anytime I had to go to the doctor, you'd dropped whatever you had going so you could fly me across the border. I took for granted how you were always there for me."

Brent shrugged. "I remember having to break a couple of hot dates because of you."

"Considering your flair for racking up females like pool balls, I figure you had to break more than a couple.

"Later on, our causing each other to hit the wall during that important race made things go from bad to worse, to my way of thinking. So when Fuelgate blew wide-open, I didn't mind one bit that the smooth ride you'd had through life was over. Finally, you were going to have to answer for what you did."

Brent felt his gut tighten. This was exactly why he hadn't wanted to discuss Fuelgate with Trey. Didn't want to see the derision in his brother's eyes. Hear him verify he believed Mike Jones's story instead of his.

"Sounds like you think I was one hell of a bad big brother."

"Yeah, I did. But it wasn't because of how you treated me." Trey retrieved his coffee, took another sip. "Bottom line is, I grew up jealous of you. Hell, deep down I knew you hadn't done what that gas man claimed. But a part of me wanted to believe you had. That way, Adam would have to kick you off the team. NASCAR wouldn't allow you to race in any of its series. For the first time in my life, I wouldn't have to compete against you on a race track. All that was totally selfish on my part."

Brent eased out a long breath. "Dad didn't do us any favors by setting us up to go against each other in everything we did."

"Agreed." Trey rose. "That doesn't excuse the fact that I wasn't there for you four years ago, defending you to NASCAR, the racing team and all the fans. Instead, I stood in the background and kept quiet."

"Considering the past, it's understandable why you did that."

"Doesn't mean I'm proud of it." Trey stuck out his hand. "I apologize. I'm here for you now, bro. In every way."

"Appreciate it."

Shaking his brother's hand, Brent felt something loosen inside of him. Only now was he willing to admit how much it had hurt when Trey distanced himself over Fuelgate while the rest of the family stood by him. And how relieved he now felt that the foundation had begun crumbling beneath the emotional barrier that had separated himself from his younger brother for so long.

Trey jabbed his fingers into the back pocket of his jeans. "When I drove away from this airport last night, I sure didn't expect to be wanting to thank Hope this morning."

Hope. Brent shoved a hand through his hair. She'd been right about his talking to Trey, he could give her that. It didn't change the fact she'd stepped over the line. "Hell," he muttered.

"Here's something else to add to my list of realizations," Trey said. "I figure the reason Hope said what she did is because she cares about you. A lot."

"Maybe so," Brent said. Just hearing that put a kink in his gut. "Doesn't change the fact she told you what I'd said in confidence. That doesn't exactly promote trust."

"There is that." Trey scrubbed at the stubble on his chin. "Remember my mentioning all those females you racked up like pool balls?"

"What about them?"

"Correct me if I'm wrong, but for you to confide in

Hope tells me she's more than just another ball on the billiard table, so to speak. So, maybe you ought to take a hard look at things and decide if the way she managed to put us on some sort of even keel for about the first time in our lives is good enough reason for you to let her get away."

THE SMELL OF RICH COFFEE mingled with smoky bacon pulled Hope out of a fitful sleep. Yawning, she tugged on a light robe over her yellow tank top and gray drawstring pants. After a stop to brush her teeth, she headed downstairs.

Last night she'd sent up silent thanks when she tiptoed past her father's bedroom and heard him snoring. After the harsh words she'd exchanged with Brent, she'd been in no condition to try to explain to her father why she was upset. She still didn't want to talk about it. Couldn't.

Just the memory of Brent looking at her with complete distrust hurt in places she hadn't known could hurt.

And there was anger, churning through the hurt.

Granted, she'd stepped over the line by pointing out to Trey that Brent had been there for him all those years ago when he'd flown him to Mexico for treatment. But it had been a small step on her part. Ninety-nine percent of her conversation with Trey had directly related to Fuelgate's effects on Sanford Racing. *Her client.* That Brent was so pigheaded he couldn't—*wouldn't*—admit that, then he had just shown himself to be the type of man she didn't care to have around.

Damn him.

Squaring her shoulders, she stepped into the kitchen. "Morning, Daddy."

Dan Hunt turned from the stove, a skillet in one hand

and a long fork in the other. As always, his thick, iron-gray hair was neatly brushed. His golf shirt and khaki pants immaculate.

He set the skillet and fork aside, crossed the kitchen in three long strides and gripped Hope's shoulders. "You want to know how scared I was when I got that call about your plane going down?"

"I was scared, too." She forced a smile. "But I should point out that we didn't crash. We merely made an emergency landing."

He wrapped his arms around her and hugged her close. "I still couldn't take a full breath until you called and told me for yourself you were okay."

Hope closed her eyes, reveling in the familiar spicy scent of his aftershave. When her work for Sanford Racing ended, it wasn't going to be easy to go back to Dallas. Maybe it was time to stop toying with the idea of relocating her company to Charlotte and get serious about it.

She inched her head back. "I'm fine. Really, I am. I'll be even better once I've had a cup of your strong-enough-to-smelt-iron coffee."

"That's the only way coffee should be made." Dan tweaked her cheek before heading back to the stove. "You're going to eat a good breakfast, too."

Hope rolled her eyes. Her father's definition of a "good breakfast" consisted of about a thousand calories. "I'll do my best."

She grabbed a thick ceramic mug out of the cabinet above the coffeemaker. After filling the mug she topped off the one her father had placed beside the stove.

Hope padded to the long, narrow island covered with a mosaic of hunter-green and terra-cotta tiles that had provided a work area for her mother's numerous cooking projects. Small pots of herbs that Linda Hunt had lovingly tended still grew on the window sills, lending their fragrance to the air. Hope knew that Grace had taken cuttings from all of the plants and now used those herbs in her own recipes.

It was comforting to know a part of her mother's legacy lived on, Hope thought as she settled on a long-legged stool. Her thoughts, as usual, drifted to the regret she felt over never having been able to convince her mother to open up about the deep-seated unhappiness Hope had sensed plagued her. And how Brent might wind up feeling that same sort of regret about his own brother.

Which was something she was not going to think about, she told herself sternly. That was Brent's problem. Not hers.

Propping her elbows on the tiles, Hope took her first sip of coffee. It was so strong it made her eyes water, but she didn't care. She welcomed the hard punch her father's brew delivered to her system.

"Tell me about the emergency landing," Dan said as he settled two plates on the island. As usual, he'd prepared enough scrambled eggs, bacon and toast to feed an entire NASCAR pit crew.

"Looking back, it wasn't so bad," she began while nibbling on a piece of bacon.

Her father ate in silence while she described what she and Brent had been through, leaving out the part where she fell asleep snuggled in his arms. And woke up realizing she'd fallen in love.

She'd been in love before, she reminded herself when her chest went tight. Got her heart broken. Bounced back. Nothing said she couldn't do that again.

His plate empty, Dan laid his fork aside. "I'd have

felt better if you'd been stranded with a man other than Brent Sanford," he said, the usual disgust sounding in his voice. "But I do give him credit for landing that plane in one piece. And keeping my baby girl safe."

If her chest got any tighter, she wasn't going to be able to breathe.

"Daddy, I want to talk to you about Fuelgate. Brent told me his version of the scandal. I'd like you to hear it."

Dan's eyes narrowed. "Are you forgetting I was crew chief for Cargill Motors when this happened?"

"Hardly. But I'm convinced the scandal has had an adverse effect on Sanford Racing's employees. My job is to help them come together as a team, and I can't do that until there's proof of what really happened. So, I'd like you to hear Brent's version."

"All right," he said, sounding far from convinced. "Tell me what Sanford said."

"He didn't pay Mike Jones to contaminate the fuel in Kent Grosso's car. Jones did it all on his own to get back at Brent."

"For what?"

"All Brent knows is what Jones told him—'I did it for *her*.' Brent has no clue who that 'her' is. Jones disappeared the day after the Talladega race, and Brent has spent the past four years trying to find him. Not even the private investigator he hired got anywhere."

Hope paused, sipped more coffee. She figured she was getting used to it since her eyes had stopped watering.

"At the last NASCAR Sprint Cup Series Awards Banquet, Uncle Alan told Adam Sanford he'd stumbled onto something that made him think Jones had set up Brent, after all. Brent wasn't at the ceremony, but he'd flown his family to New York, so Uncle Alan scheduled a time the following day to talk to Adam and Brent about what he'd found out. But he was murdered that night."

Hope saw a flicker in her father's eyes that had her own eyes narrowing. "Do you know something about Mike Jones? Do you know where he is?"

"No." Dan shoved a hand through his gray hair. "But Alan mentioned something about Jones's ex-wife the last time he called me."

Hope's heartbeat picked up speed as she took her father's hand in hers. "What about her?"

"Alan ran into her in Florida while he was there on his annual fishing trip." Dan tapped a stubby fingertip against the counter top. "You know, he and I had gone fishing there every year since we met. It was our post-season tradition. I didn't go this last time because I'd lost your mother and just didn't feel up to it. Figured Alan and I would make the trip together after NASCAR's season ended this year."

Hope heard the elusive sadness in her father's voice, and squeezed his hand tighter. "You lost two people you loved only months apart. I wish I could do something to help ease the pain."

"Only time will do that, baby girl."

Hope nodded. Years ago, illness had claimed his first wife, Ethan and Jared's mother. Dan Hunt knew all about the stages of grief.

"Daddy, what exactly did Uncle Alan say about Mike Jones's ex-wife?"

"Just that he'd stopped for a drink at our favorite watering hole and struck up a conversation with one of the female bartenders. He told her he owned a NASCAR team, was getting ready to sell it and retire.

The woman said her ex-husband had been an over-the-wall guy a few years ago, but had gotten fired. Turns out, she'd been married to Mike Jones after he left NASCAR. She told Alan that Mike had bragged about getting back at the bastards during the time he worked in NASCAR."

"Did she tell Uncle Alan what he'd done?"

"If she did, he didn't say. And he didn't mention anything to me about his thinking Sanford had been set up. Maybe that's because when Alan called he was at the Miami airport, in a rush to get to the gate." Dan scrubbed a hand over his face. "He was murdered a couple of days later. All thoughts of that call just went out of my head."

"Understandable." Hope pulled her cell phone out of the pocket of her robe. "What's the name of the bar Jones's ex worked at?"

"Double Dave's. It's near the Haulover Marina in North Miami Beach."

"Double Dave's?"

Dan shrugged. "It's owned by two guys, both named Dave."

"Original," she murmured, using her phone to access the Internet. She found the listing for the bar, called it.

"Yo, this is Dave." The man's voice resonated with a nicotine huskiness.

"Hi, this is Hope Hunt. My uncle stopped by your bar last winter and struck up a conversation with one of your bartenders. I don't know her name, but she used to be married to a guy named Mike Jones."

"That'd be Violet. Violet Jones. She quit a few months back."

"Do you have a phone number or address where I can reach her? Or her ex-husband?"

"Nope. I don't keep track of employees after they move on." He paused, then added, "Seems like I heard Violet was bartending down in Key West."

"Any idea what bar?"

"Nope."

Hope's next call was to directory assistance. There was no listing for a Violet Jones in Key West.

"Almost thirty variations of the name Mike Jones popped up," she told her father after she hung up. "And a whole slew of 'M. Jones.'" Hope felt each individual pulse point in her body throb in frustration. "*The* Mike Jones might be one of them. Or none. And it's a guess whether he even has a land line. He maybe just uses a cell phone."

"Baby girl, your hands are shaking."

And her stomach was churning. "Finding Mike Jones and getting the truth out of him is important to the job I'm doing for Sanford Racing."

"It's important to Brent Sanford, too."

"Yes," Hope agreed. "If he can clear his name, I'm sure he'll be able to move right on with his life." Or so he thinks.

Dan's eyes sharpened on her face. "He matters, doesn't he? Sanford matters to you."

Dammit, the last thing she had intended was to wear her battered heart on her sleeve.

"I believe he's innocent," she said vaguely.

Dan pursed his mouth. "Well, if Mike Jones did lie, it sounds like he messed with a lot of people."

"An understatement." Hope checked the clock on the wall, then slid off of her stool. "I'm going to Sanford Racing. If Adam agrees with what I want to do, I won't be home tonight. Maybe for a few nights."

"Where will you be?"

"Key West." She pressed a kiss to her father's temple. "First thing on my list is finding Violet Jones. The second is tracking down her lying ex-husband."

CHAPTER TWELVE

Clad in hot-pink capris and a sleeveless top, her strappy sandals clicking against the wooden walkway, Hope stepped into the Parrot's Cove bar. Although the thatched roof establishment billed itself as a one-of-a-kind open-air tropical saloon, it resembled a handful of the bars she'd made the rounds of since she arrived in Key West two days ago. Truth was, she'd visited so many she was beginning to recognize some of the sunburned tourists who were apparently engaging in their own version of barhopping.

She, however, was on a mission.

Until late last night, none of the locals she'd talked to knew Violet Jones. Or her ex-husband, Mike. Then she'd ducked into one last club on the way back to her hotel, and struck gold. A bartender with uncountable tattoos advised that Violet Jones had worked there for a few months. If memory served him right, she'd moved on to a job at the Parrot's Cove.

Now, armed with a description of Violet, Hope squinted against the sun's reflection off the open expanse of the Atlantic. A breeze carrying the salty scent of the sea wafted through the bar while she swept her gaze around its interior that featured a wooden floor, bamboo-looking fixtures and fake parrots perched in equally fake trees. A good hour before lunchtime, only one table was inhabited by three men wearing bright tropical shirts and drinking Bloody Marys. A lone male sat at the bar, nursing a beer.

Just when Hope began wondering if any waitstaff were actually on duty, a door behind the bar swung open. A tall woman clad in a white T-shirt and jeans, blond hair in short spikes, stepped into view.

Hope's heart shot into her throat. The bartender she'd talked to last night had told her Violet Jones was as skinny as a broomstick. He'd been right.

"Get you something?" the woman asked as Hope slid onto a bar stool.

Up close, Hope noted a small army of multicolored loops marching up the curve of her left ear. "A Virgin Mary, extra spicy, and some information."

Without comment, the woman settled a napkin on the bar, its gleaming wood nearly black with age. A moment later, she placed a tall glass of tomato juice sprouting a spear of celery on the napkin. "What sort of information?"

"For starters, I need to make sure you're Violet Jones."

"That's me." Her eyes narrowed. "Do I know you?"

"No, my name's Hope Hunt. My uncle, Alan Cargill, stopped by Double Dave's last winter, and struck up a conversation with you."

"Cargill. Cargill…that name sounds familiar."

"He owned a NASCAR race team, was getting ready to sell it and retire."

"Oh, *him*." Violet scrubbed a hand across the back of her neck. "Small world, you know? For my ex's former boss to show up in the bar where I worked."

"I understand you told him before your ex-husband

got fired he'd bragged about getting back at the bastards while he worked for Cargill Motors."

"Look, I shouldn't have said anything. Mike and I had just had another big blowup, and I was pissed."

Hope sipped her drink. It was cold and spicy and hit the spot. "I'd like to know what else you told Alan Cargill that night."

"Nothing else. He didn't hang around long because he had to catch a plane. Said he'd be in touch, but I never heard back from him." Violet arched a blond brow. "Since he's your uncle, why don't you just ask him?"

"I wish I could. He was murdered in December."

"That's awful," Violet said, her expression instantly softening. "I hope the cops got whoever did it."

"They haven't yet." Talking about the murder sent a wave of quiet sorrow through Hope. "Have you ever heard of Brent Sanford?"

Violet shook her head. "Doesn't ring a bell."

"He's the driver your ex-husband decided to pay back. Apparently Sanford somehow hurt a woman who meant something to Mike. Because of that, Sanford had to quit the NASCAR circuit. His family's racing team has suffered. It's still not back on a steady keel. I'm here to find out Mike's motive for what he did."

"Why? Why does it matter to you?"

"I'm a team-building consultant. Brent Sanford is a…" Hope hesitated. Just thinking about him put a knot in her stomach. They hadn't spoken since that night at the airport. She'd considered calling him more than once. Then thought better of it. She had apologized, after all. Told him she genuinely regretted the one small slip she'd made to Trey. *One small slip.* As far as she was concerned, the next move was Brent's. And if he chose not to make one, well, she would deal with that when the time came.

"Brent Sanford is a what?" Violet prodded.

"Acquaintance. Sanford Racing is my client. Mike admitted to Brent that he'd set him up because of some woman. I'm trying to find out who she is."

Violet shifted her gaze out the paneless windows to the ocean where wave swallowed wave. "A team-building consultant," she said after a moment. "Like, what do you do?"

Hope tried to swallow her impatience. She hadn't come there to chat about what she did for a living. But she needed Violet's cooperation, and being short with her wouldn't get her what she needed. "I help employees learn to work together efficiently. Build confidence in each other. Trust."

"You ever lend a hand at putting marriages back together?"

The pain that had settled in the woman's eyes erased Hope's impatience. "I haven't yet. There's always a first time."

Retrieving a rag from beneath the counter, Violet began scrubbing the already gleaming wood. "I'll tell you what I know because it has totally wrecked my marriage. I'm sick of having it hanging over us." Her voice hitched. "If it gets out in the open, maybe things will change for Mike and me."

"I'm listening," Hope said quietly.

"His mother. The woman Mike wanted to avenge was his mother."

Hope blinked. "His *mother?*"

The customer at the end of the bar snagged Violet's attention. "Be back."

Frowning, Hope watched her move away. During his racing years, Brent had been photographed with a bevy of women, all his age or younger. She wasn't sure how old Mike Jones was, but surely his mother would be around the same age as Kath Sanford. What the heck could Brent have done to Mrs. Jones that would prompt such revenge by her son?

"Want another drink?" Violet asked after she'd served the customer at the bar, then carried a tray of refills to the men dressed in bright topical shirts.

"No, thanks. I'd like to hear about Mike's mother."

Violet picked up a paring knife and began slicing a lime. "His dad took off when Mike was a baby, so it was just him and his mom, Nola. When Mike was in his early teens, she fell crazy in love with a race car driver. The guy took Mike under his wing, shared his love of cars and racing. From the sound of things, he was the first male who'd spent any quality time with Mike and he drank it all in like water."

"How does that relate to what happened at Talladega four years ago?"

"Turns out, Nola's squeeze had a wife and sons. Mike's dream of the guy becoming his stepdad ended when he keeled over from a heart attack while he and Nola were on a chartered fishing trip. The boat's captain was a huge NASCAR fan. He recognized the driver, knew it wasn't his wife he'd chartered the boat with. The captain tipped off some sports reporter the instant he got back to the dock."

"Wild Bobby Sanford," Hope murmured.

Violet lifted a shoulder. "Mike never told me the driver's name. And I don't follow NASCAR, so I had no clue who he was talking about."

The information Violet had imparted had Hope's mind racing. "I understand how awful Wild Bobby's death must have been for Mike. But why would he blame Brent Sanford for that?"

"He didn't, not for the affair. It was what happened after Wild Bobby died."

"Go on."

"According to Mike, Nola viewed her life as empty without the man she loved. She went into a deep depression, lost her job and started drinking. Mike tried to help her, but all she wanted was to wallow in her grief. And all he could do was watch her. She died a couple of years later."

Violet's mouth thinned as she put more muscle behind slicing the lime. "That's when Mike vowed to get even with the man's family. The way he saw it, this Wild Bobby guy had broken his mother's heart and wrecked his own dreams. Why shouldn't theirs get totaled, too? Mike got a job at a race track. He swept floors for anyone who would hire him. Worked seven days a week in the hopes of winning a spot on a pit crew. Finally he did."

Hope shook her head, incredulous. "That must have taken years."

"Didn't matter to Mike. Putting himself in the position to avenge his mother did. It was like a quest." Violet grabbed another lime and went at it with her knife. "I didn't know about any of that until after Mike and I were married awhile. One night we got tanked on margaritas and he told me what he'd done. I wish to hell he hadn't."

"Why?"

"He sounded so damn smug about the whole thing.

It made me sick to my stomach to learn he'd taken so much joy in hurting that driver's family. I told him how I felt, but it didn't seem to sink in. After that, nothing between us was the same. We started fighting." She dumped a pile of lime slices in a bowl. "We lived in Miami, then. When I left him, he moved down here."

Hope's pulse kicked up a notch. "He's here? Mike lives in Key West?"

Violet nodded. "We started calling each other a few months ago. Trying to work things out. After we talked a couple of times, Mike admitted that maybe I was right and he'd gone too far trying to even the score. He sounded like he meant it." She shrugged. "I moved down here to see how it goes between us. Might have been the stupidest thing I've ever done, but here I am."

Her training kicking in, Hope forced her breathing to stay even. Granted, she was emotionally involved, but letting her emotions guide her now as she had done during her conversation with Trey would be a mistake.

"When Nola got involved with Wild Bobby, Mike was at a very impressionable age," she began. "So, it's understandable that he suffered when his dreams died along with the man he viewed as a father figure. Add to that, Mike endured years of watching his mother suffer. But that doesn't excuse what he did to the Sanford family. Mike needs to make things right."

Violet looked at the bar's entrance where several customers had appeared. "The lunch crush is about to start. I've given you all the time I have right now."

"And I appreciate it," Hope said. "I'm going to call Brent Sanford and tell him what you told me. I imagine he'll want to chat with Mike in person."

Violet stabbed her fingers through her spiky hair. "Mike'll hate me for the rest of his life for talking to you."

"If so, that will be his loss. Brent has spent four years in hell. He had to rebuild his life from the ground up, and he has a right to face his accuser." Hope heard emotion break through in her voice, but she couldn't help it. "He deserves the truth. As does Sanford Racing. And NASCAR."

Violet gave her a long, steady look. "I've tended bar a long time. Customers pour out their hearts on a regular basis. So, I've got a knack for spotting someone who's hurting. Sounds to me like you and Sanford are more than just acquaintances."

Hope lifted her chin. Dammit, she hated that she was so easy to read.

"I need to know where your ex-husband works."

Violet crossed her arms over her chest. "Look, I agree that it's time Mike faces up to what he's done. But he's not going to have to do that without me."

Hope narrowed her eyes. "The instant I leave here, you could pick up the phone and call Mike. Warn him that he's going to get a visit from Brent Sanford. If you do that, there's a chance Mike might take off. Maybe disappear on you, too."

"Yeah, that could happen if I planned to warn Mike. I don't. He needs to face what he did." As if accepting fate, Violet eased out a breath. "If what I've done ruins things between him and me, I'll deal with it."

Hope knew it was possible Violet could be lying about not tipping off Mike. Still, instinct told her the woman was telling the truth. "The conversation between Brent and Mike probably won't be pleasant. Are you sure you want to be there?"

"Having my marriage fall apart over this deal wasn't pleasant, either. It's time to put it to rest. Give the Sanfords their due. I just want to be there when you and the guy who apparently matters a whole lot to you confront Mike."

Hope gave a mental nod to Violet's astuteness. And cemented her determination to do a better job at hiding her feelings.

"All right." She laid money on the bar, then rose. "Give me your phone number. I'll let you know when Brent plans to arrive."

OVER THE PAST TWO DAYS, Brent had dealt with so many frustrations, he'd lost count. Hope topped the list. Followed by the storm system off Alaska's coast that had morphed into a hellish blizzard, then switched direction without warning. Vicious wind and blinding snow had forced him to set the Lear down at an airstrip two hundred miles from the hunting lodge where the CEO buddies had reservations. The dot-on-the-map town nearest the airstrip had one hotel. A single café. Zilch cell phone service. The landline shared by the hotel and café was filled with so much static that hearing anyone on the other end proved impossible.

Doggedly, he kept telling himself it was just as well he couldn't put a call through to Hope. Hadn't he convinced himself he needed a chance to cool off? Time to figure out just how deep his feelings for her went?

But when he lay in bed at night, he imagined what it would be like to have her with him beneath the sheets, her soft, warm flesh pressed against his. That image restarted the painfully sexy dreams that had plagued him when he first met her. He couldn't stop thinking about her. Wishing for her. *Wanting her.*

Two miserable days later the weather cleared enough so he could get the Lear and his passengers back into the air. By then, he'd been raw with frustration, both professional and personal. The professional reasons were obvious—when weather grounded one of his planes, his company's bottom line suffered. The personal reasons were more obscure, but they'd hit him with the force of a sledgehammer.

Where Hope was concerned, he hadn't just been circling close to the *L* word. He'd fallen all the way in love with her. When, he had no clue. It didn't matter he hadn't known her for long. He knew what was in his heart. Trey had been right—she was special. *The one.* Smart, funny, gorgeous. Hell, even her damn meddling had a singular effect on him.

Just the idea that he'd totally blown their relationship and she might refuse to see him again had true fear roaring through his veins. He was willing to do whatever it took to make things right.

The instant his passengers deplaned for the hunting lodge, he turned on his cell phone, checked for messages. And felt a wave of relief when he saw Hope had called. Just hearing her recorded voice had the same power as a punch in the gut. Then her words sunk in, leaving him slack jawed.

She'd found Mike Jones!

How the hell had she managed to locate the man in two days when *he'd* spent four years hunting the bastard?

Not until Brent listened to her message for a third time did he snap to the tone in Hope's voice. No excitement. No warmth. Just coolly businesslike. The message might just as well have been delivered by a total stranger.

Yeah, he'd blown things, all right.

He heard confirmation of that in her voice when he returned her call. With stubborn perversity, she'd kept their conversation focused on how she had tracked down Violet Jones, and what the woman had told her. Although he'd been close to speechless over hearing that Fuelgate had been all about Mike Jones taking revenge because of Wild Bobby's relationship with Mike's mother, Brent had managed to bring up the issue of *them*. Without hesitation, Hope changed the subject, then ended the call.

He'd filed a flight plan for Key West, cursing the entire time he sat behind the Lear's controls.

He was still cursing when his cab braked in front of the Parrot's Cove bar where Hope had told him to meet her.

Brent added a tip to the cabbie's fare, then climbed out into the warm tropical sunshine at the same time Hope walked out of the bar.

Just the sight of her kicked up his pulse rate. She wore a big pair of black sunglasses, black capris and a sleeveless coral top that made her skin glow. A breeze that carried the scent of the sea ruffled her dark hair.

"Captain Sanford," she said smoothly.

Because he was tempted to reach for her, he shoved his hands into the pockets of his slacks. "Doc. Good to see you."

She pointed toward the bar with her chin. "Violet Jones works here. She'll be out in a minute to take us to see her ex-husband."

"Where is he?"

"At work. Violet won't tell me where. I think she's afraid I'll go see him on my own."

"Look, Hope—"

She held up a hand. "There are some things we need to go over before we see Mike."

"All right." He would let her put him off, but only for so long.

"I don't know if you've talked to Adam lately—"

"I haven't."

"Then I want you to understand that I'm here representing Sanford Racing." Despite the designer sunglasses, he caught the pointed look she sent him. "I'm not trying to 'fix' you or interfere in your life in any way."

But she had interfered. Immensely. And he had no intention of going back to the way things had been before she first climbed into the cockpit of his plane. The only future he wanted was with her.

"Understood. Hope—"

"I feel I should add that if we're reasonable, we can keep this uncomplicated."

Her cool attitude was steadily feeding his temper. He stepped closer, dipped his head and drew in her seductive scent. "No."

She lifted her chin to meet his gaze, putting their mouths only inches apart. "No, what?"

"No, I don't want to be reasonable, and it's already complicated," he grated through his teeth. "I want to have a chat with Mike Jones in the worst way. But more importantly, you and I need to talk."

"Sorry to keep you waiting."

Brent glanced past Hope's shoulder, saw a tall woman dressed in a pink T-shirt and jeans. She was as skinny as an eel, with a hard, suspicious face and bright blond hair worn in spikes. Multicolored studs rode up the curve of her left ear.

"VIOLET JONES, THIS IS BRENT Sanford," Hope said, careful to keep her voice conversational. Had she honestly believed she could see Brent and feel nothing? With her pulse hammering in her ears, it was clear she'd been wrong.

But she would get through this.

Her gaze on Brent, Violet stabbed her fingers into the back pocket of her jeans. "I could tell you that Mike was wrong to do what he did to you. But I don't guess that would help."

"It doesn't. I appreciate the thought, though."

Hope turned to Violet. "Do we need to get a cab to go to where Mike works?"

"No." Violet pointed down the street. "He's a mechanic. At that garage."

Hope followed Violet's gaze. The garage was a blue-aluminum-sided rectangle squeezed in between a bar and a convenience store.

"Let's get this done," Brent said.

When he placed a hand under her elbow, Hope was tempted to pull away. But his touch felt so good against her bare flesh. *So right.*

As they neared the garage, Hope saw that it had three bays, the overhead doors all raised. A car sat in each bay; two up on hydraulic lifts, another sat on the oil-splotched floor with its hood raised. A mechanic wearing a navy jumpsuit was bent over the engine.

Violet inclined her head. "That's Mike."

"Is there a place where we can talk in private?" Brent asked.

She nodded. "They've got a picnic table out back. The guys eat lunch there."

"That'll do." Brent's mouth settled into a grim line. "Either you get him out there, or I will."

"I'll do it," Violet said, nerves sounding in her voice.

When Brent tightened his fingers on Hope's elbow, she could feel the tension pulsing inside him. "We'll meet you out there."

The lunch area consisted of the single picnic table bolted to a concrete patio. A plastic garbage can sat nearby. A couple of palm trees provided small islands of shade.

"It still hasn't sunk in that this is happening," Brent said, his dark gaze meeting hers. "I understand you didn't track him down for me, but I want to thank you." His eyes softened and he lowered his voice. "And also for what you said to Trey. He came to see me that next morning. We talked. For the first time in our lives, we really talked. It felt good."

Hope's emotions, that had hovered on edge for days, teetered. Since she had no idea how to respond, she was thankful that Violet and Mike Jones stepped out on the patio at that moment.

"Dammit." Mike came to a dead halt when his gaze landed on Brent. "What the hell are you doing here?"

Hope took in the man who had been hurt so badly and caused others so much pain. He was six feet of solid muscle with a linebacker's shoulders. His blond hair was drawn back in a ponytail with a leather thong. He was so tan that his blue eyes seemed to blaze in his square-jawed face.

"I intend to hear the truth about Talladega come out of your mouth," Brent answered, his hands curling into fists against his thighs. "You can confess willingly, or I'll force it. Either way, I'm going to get it."

Mike's belligerent gaze whipped to Hope. "Who are you?"

"Dr. Hunt. I represent Sanford Racing. I'm also interested in hearing only the truth."

He whirled toward his ex-wife, his face lit with fury. "What the hell have you done?"

"I'm not the one who *did* things," she snapped out, stabbing a finger at his chest. "You set all this in motion. You did wrong, and you know it. I can't stand to think about what harm you did to this man and his family. And how smug you sounded when you told me about it. You claim you still love me. That you want us back together. It's time to prove that. Because if you don't step up and take responsibility, then you and I don't have a future. Period."

Hope noted the angry red that washed beneath the man's skin. Beneath the jumpsuit, his chest rose and fell at a rapid rate. But something lurked in his molten blue eyes, the shadow of a shadow. "I don't want to lose you again, Vi."

"Then don't." She waved an unsteady hand toward Brent. "Talk to him. Tell him the truth about your mom and why you set him up."

His jaw working tensely, Mike jerked a rag out of his back pocket, began scrubbing his grease-streaked hands. After a moment he blew out a breath. Then another.

He shifted his gaze back to Brent. "Guess I'd rather talk to you than fight you."

"Works for me. As long as what you tell me is the truth."

BRENT STEPPED TO THE PICNIC table, swept a hand toward the opposite side, indicating Jones take a seat across from him. *Facing him.*

Mike did so. It took only a second for Violet to slide in beside her ex-husband.

Brent stared into the man's face and felt hate. It was liquid and cold, like mercury flowing through his veins. The bastard had upended his life and stolen parts of it he could never get back. *Never.*

"I'm listening."

Mike stared down at the rag now clenched in both of his hands. "I don't remember my dad, he took off when I was little. My mom dated lots of guys. Most were losers. But when I was in my early teens, she brought Wild Bobby Sanford home. He was different. He didn't act like I was just a kid who was getting in his way like most of the others guys she saw. He listened to what I said. Acted like my opinion meant something. For the first time in my life, I knew what it was like to have a dad.

"At first, I didn't know Wild Bobby already had a wife. Didn't know about you and your brothers. I thought we had him all to ourselves."

Brent looked away. He'd grown up watching his mother endure the pain from his father's numerous affairs. Mike's mother would have just been another in a long line of women.

"Go on," he urged.

"Wild Bobby taught me all about racing. He showed me how to work on a car's engine. Took me to football games. And he was good to my mom. Even if I'd known he was married, I wouldn't have cared. Because before he came around, my life was in shadows. Wild Bobby was like the sun. Then he died, and everything went dark again."

Brent scrubbed a hand across his face. He knew exactly what Jones was talking about. There'd been an

electrifying intensity to the father who'd been boister-
ous, disrespectful of rules and enduringly upbeat.
Bigger than life, had been the way Brent had viewed
him. And, despite the circumstances of his death, losing
his father had settled a black core of grief at the center
of his being.

"My mom suffered after that," Mike continued, his
voice sounding like rusted metal. "Obviously she
couldn't even go to Wild Bobby's funeral. She started
drinking. A lot. Lost her job as a waitress. We were so
damn broke. No health insurance. No money in the
bank. Nothing. We sold everything we owned. *Everything*—the car, furniture, jewelry that'd been my
grandma's. I worked odd jobs after school trying to
keep my mom afloat, but life kept kicking both of us in
the teeth. A couple of years after Bobby died, so did she.
It was like she just gave up. The doctors called it a heart
attack. I called it a broken heart. Nobody cared that
she'd lost her illicit lover."

Emotion delivered a hard, bruising punch to Brent's
chest. "My mother suffered, too. You think it was easy
for her, knowing her husband died while with his
mistress?" He didn't realize his voice echoed the
rawness inside him until Hope settled beside him and
laid a palm over his arm.

"Mike," she began softly, "everyone understands that
you and your mother suffered after Wild Bobby died.
Even so, that doesn't excuse what you did to Brent and
his family."

"I was mad," he snapped. "Wanted to get back at
someone. Thinking about getting revenge is what got
me through after my mom died." He used a forearm to
swipe the sweat off his brow, then shifted his gaze back

to Brent. "After I set you up at Talladega, I wouldn't let myself think about what I'd done. I just got on with my life. Met Vi and fell in love with her." He darted a look at his ex-wife. "When I told Vi about how I'd set you up, that ruined things for us."

Brent studied the woman with short, spiky hair whose eyes brimmed with tears. He'd seen his own mother cry an ocean over his father's numerous infidelities.

He looked back at Jones. "You'll understand why you won't get any sympathy from me on that score."

"Yeah." Something that looked a lot like genuine remorse drew the man's face into a stark mask. "I'm sorry for what I did at Talladega. To you. And your family."

"Your apology is only the first thing I want," Brent said evenly. "There's more."

Jones eased out a resigned breath. "NASCAR?"

"NASCAR," Brent echoed. "I want them to hear the truth from you. Their headquarters is in Daytona. My Lear's at the airport. We can be there in a couple of hours."

Mike shrugged. "Gotta check with my boss before I leave."

"I'm going, too." Violet squeezed his hand, then looked at Brent. "Please let me go."

"All right. But I'll be flying home after that." Brent paused. He was angry at Jones, but the man was willing to face up to what he'd done. "I've got a pilot friend who has a plane hangared in Daytona. I'll call and see if he can fly you back here."

While Mike went to talk to his boss, Brent looked at Hope. They might as well have been sitting at a poker table for all he could tell from her expression.

"Are you coming to Daytona?" he asked quietly.

"Yes. My client will want a full report on what happens at NASCAR headquarters."

"Good. It just so happens I need a navigator. Seems you're the only one who knows how to keep me on course."

CHAPTER THIRTEEN

LATE THAT AFTERNOON, HOPE SLID a sideways look at Brent across the backseat of their taxi heading toward Daytona Beach International Airport. He seemed lost in thought, his profile hard and unyielding.

"Now that Mike Jones has come clean with NASCAR, I doubt it will take long for you to get the go-ahead to return to racing," she said. "If that's what you want to do."

Instead of replying, he leaned forward and said to the driver, "Stop at the resort coming up on the left."

"Resort?" The taxi made a sharp enough turn that Hope had to grip the armrest. Ahead of them, the sun streaked the ocean with ribbons of orange. "I thought we were going to the airport."

"We are. Eventually." He shifted back on the seat. "Since we missed lunch, we ought to eat something first." His eyes stayed steady on hers. "We need to talk, Hope. I don't want to do that while sitting at the controls of the Lear."

Nerves tightened her stomach. "The last time we had a conversation, things didn't turn out so well," she said cautiously.

BRENT SAW THE UNEASINESS in her eyes that sounded in her voice. The past days had given him a preview of what his life would be without her. He was prepared to do battle if she told him to take a hike.

"That particular chat didn't turn out well," he agreed. "Even so, Dr. Hunt, after your sweeping endorsement of the value of conversation, I didn't think you'd run from one."

"I'm not running." Her forehead furrowed. "Maybe retreating a little."

He'd hurt her by telling her he didn't trust her. It was no wonder she'd taken a step back. Maybe more than just one.

"So, how about we compromise? I talk. You listen." He offered her his hand as the taxi braked to a halt. "I'd appreciate it if you'd at least hear me out."

She hesitated before slipping her hand into his. "Well, I *am* hungry."

A stone walkway offered a route through lush gardens and a carpet of sloping green lawn that spilled down to the beach. The sand was dotted with people, umbrellas and lounge chairs. They passed a poolside restaurant, moving toward a set of marble stairs that led to the resort's main building.

"We're not eating out here?" she asked.

"No. The restaurant has terrace dining." He escorted her inside toward the hostess's pedestal. "Sanford," he told the woman wearing a starched white blouse and slim black skirt.

Hope looked up at him through her lashes. "When did you make reservations?"

"I called while we were at NASCAR headquarters. You were still on the phone to Adam."

Moments later they were seated at the edge of the terrace. A warm breeze rustled the coconut palms that hugged the beach.

"Nice view," she said, looking past the gardens to the sea.

"The best," Brent agreed, keeping his gaze on her face. Just looking at her overwhelmed him. Made him ache. Made him want even more what he wasn't certain he could have.

"I won my first NASCAR Sprint Cup Series race in Daytona," he said. "Afterward, I came here to celebrate. That was a momentous day for me. It changed my life."

"The same goes for today," she said before sipping her water.

"It could." Everything depended on her.

"Could? Having your name cleared with NASCAR and everyone associated with racing is huge."

"It means a lot," he agreed. The waiter who'd seated them returned with the bottle of champagne Brent had ordered. "For now, just pour a glass for the lady," he instructed.

"For now?" Hope asked after the waiter settled the bottle in the cooler he'd placed beside the table, then moved away. She sipped from her flute. "You can't have champagne, then fly a plane."

"Whether I have a drink later, or not, is up to you."

"If you have a drink, we'll have to stay in Daytona Beach tonight."

"Also true."

She watched him behind the rim of her glass. "I don't think that would be a good idea, considering."

Because he wasn't sure how to say what needed to be said, he shifted his gaze to the sea.

"I once had what I thought was the perfect life," he began. "A career I loved. Plenty of women to keep me company. It all seemed ideal. Then Fuelgate happened and everything came crashing down around me."

He looked back at her. Her expression was absolutely still. Absolutely unreadable. "It's almost surreal to think that the lies Mike Jones told that day at Talladega are the reason Adam hired you four years later to get his team back on track."

"And it was just simple luck that you told me Mike Jones claimed one of the guys on the team set up the supposed meet between you two. Otherwise, I doubt I would have ever snapped to the fact that the distrust some of Adam's guys have for each other links all the way back to Fuelgate."

"Seems like trust issues are playing a big part in this, all the way around. I trusted you not to say anything to Trey, but you did."

"And I apologized for that."

"Yes, you did. Thoroughly."

She set her glass aside. "It's no excuse, but I couldn't convince my mother to tell me her secret. She carried it to the grave, and I regret every day I didn't do more to try to get her to confide in me. I didn't want you to regret not talking to Trey about Fuelgate." Emotion flickered in her gray eyes. "I never meant to betray your trust."

"I know that. I also know that if you hadn't said anything, Trey never would have shown up in my office the following morning. And he and I wouldn't have gotten a lot of things out in the open that needed to get out." He reached across the small table for her hand, linked his fingers with hers. "You hit a nerve, Hope. You made me face a lot of things I thought I should keep under lock and key, and I'm grateful."

"I'm just glad things worked out between you and Trey."

"So am I. But my baby brother isn't my major concern right now. You are. I acted like a stubborn idiot when all you were trying to do was help me, and I hurt you. I've no excuse for it and I'm truly sorry." As though he expected her to bolt from the table, he tightened his fingers on hers. "It was an incredibly stupid thing for a man to do to the woman he loves."

HER LIPS TREMBLED OPEN. Her heart began to beat in a quick, almost painful rhythm. "You...what?"

"It was a surprise to me, too," he murmured. "The tricky thing about life is that too often you don't know what's important until the moment passes. Thanks to that damn Alaskan blizzard that grounded my plane, I found out what it'd be like to be cut off from you totally. To not have you in my life. I don't ever want that to happen again."

"Brent—"

"No, let me finish. There are things I need to say to you."

"All right." She slicked her tongue across her lips that had gone bone-dry. "Go on."

"I never wanted to feel this way about anyone and it's been easy to avoid it until you. It means strings, and responsibilities, and it means maybe I can live my life without you, but I'd never be whole. Not without you with me." His voice softened. "I love you, Hope Hunt. I want to spend the rest of my life with you."

"I...need to catch my breath" was all she could say. Rocked by the knowledge he had so much feeling for her in him, she rose and walked the few shaky steps to the edge of the terrace. Her pulse hammered, her vision turned bleary with tears.

Brent was beside her instantly. "Don't cry." He placed his hands on her shoulders, nudged her around to face him. "Doc, it isn't doing much for my ego to tell you I love you, then to watch you break out in tears."

"I'm not crying." She sniffed. Blinked. "I just got something in my eyes, is all."

"If you say so." Looking unconvinced, he slid his hands down her arms, grazed his fingertips along her hands before he released her.

"This is all so sudden. Unexpected."

"You'll get no argument from me." He leaned against the railing that edged the terrace. "So, what are we going to do about all this?"

"I don't know." She raked an unsteady hand through her hair. "When we met, I thought you were a liar and a cheat, just like my rat-faced ex-fiancé. The last thing I wanted was to care about you. But how could I not when you scoured the continent just to find a toy NASCAR race car for a little boy's birthday? Then I found out how you risked your own life to save the parachutist whose lines got tangled on your plane." She poked a finger at his chest. "Dammit, Brent Sanford, things would have been a lot easier if you weren't such a good guy."

He used the side of one of his own fingers to nudge her chin up. "Would it help if I apologize? Say I'm sorry I'm not more like the rat-faced guy?"

She waved him off. "All along I believed what was between us meant more to me than it did to you. That falling in love with you was a huge risk for me to take because it was all one-sided."

He grabbed her hands, gripping hard. "You love me?"

"I didn't want to because you're stubborn, really pig-headed. But, yes, I do."

He smiled down at her. "It's happened."

"What?"

"This day has just officially become momentous."

"Don't get ahead of yourself. I'm the doctor here." She tugged from his hold. "Things don't get momentous until I say they do."

"Meaning?" he asked.

"Are you really going to be okay with this? If we're together, I expect to be able to talk to you about anything. And for you to not try to evade the subject. You won't always like it. *I* won't always like it, but it has to be that way."

"I agree."

"I want a partner, someone I trust no matter what and I want that person to trust me the same way."

"That's what I want, too. And I want it to be you."

A sweet, vicarious joy rushed through Hope as she moved back to the table and plucked the champagne bottle from the cooler. Her hands were trembling so badly, the champagne sloshed as she topped off her own flute, then filled his.

Returning to him, she offered him a glass. And amazed herself when her voice didn't betray the crazy pounding of her heart. "I prescribe a toast."

He lifted a brow as he took the glass from her hand. "Dr. Hunt, do you understand if I drink this it officially grounds us here for the night? Together."

"Yes."

He dipped his head. "If we stay, there's no way we're going to spend the night fully clothed in the plane's baggage compartment."

His breath washed over her cheek, sending a warm, delicious sizzle of anticipation through her.

"Oh, really?" she murmured. "What will we be doing?"

"Loving each other. Tonight and forever."

Her heart melted. "Forever?"

He tapped the rim of her glass against his. The crystal sang on the warm, tropical breeze. "You can bank on it."

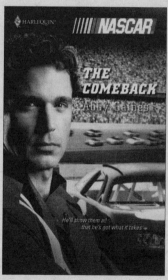

REQUEST YOUR FREE BOOKS!

2 FREE RIVETING INSPIRATIONAL NOVELS
PLUS 2 FREE MYSTERY GIFTS

YES! Please send me 2 FREE Love Inspired® Suspense novels and my 2 FREE mystery gifts (gifts are worth about $10). After receiving them, if I don't wish to receive any more books, I can return the shipping statement marked "cancel". If I don't cancel, I will receive 4 brand-new novels every month and be billed just $4.24 per book in the U.S. or $4.74 per book in Canada. That's a savings of over 20% off the cover price. It's quite a bargain! Shipping and handling is just 50¢ per book.* I understand that accepting the 2 free books and gifts places me under no obligation to buy anything. I can always return a shipment and cancel at any time. Even if I never buy another book, the two free books and gifts are mine to keep forever.

123 IDN EYM2   323 IDN EYNE

Name _____ (PLEASE PRINT) _____

Address _____ Apt. # _____

City _____ State/Prov. _____ Zip/Postal Code _____

Signature (if under 18, a parent or guardian must sign) _____

Mail to Steeple Hill Reader Service:
IN U.S.A.: P.O. Box 1867, Buffalo, NY 14240-1867
IN CANADA: P.O. Box 609, Fort Erie, Ontario L2A 5X3

Not valid to current subscribers of Love Inspired Suspense books.

Want to try two free books from another series?
Call 1-800-873-8635 or visit www.morefreebooks.com

* Terms and prices subject to change without notice. Prices do not include applicable taxes. Sales tax applicable in N.Y. Canadian residents will be charged applicable provincial taxes and GST. Offer not valid in Quebec. This offer is limited to one order per household. All orders subject to approval. Credit or debit balances in a customer's account(s) may be offset by any other outstanding balance owed by or to the customer. Please allow 4 to 6 weeks for delivery. Offer available while quantities last.

Your Privacy: Steeple Hill Books is committed to protecting your privacy. Our Privacy Policy is available online at www.SteepleHill.com or upon request from the Reader Service. From time to time we make our lists of customers available to reputable third parties who may have a product or service of interest to you. If you would prefer we not share your name and address, please check here. ☐

LISUS09

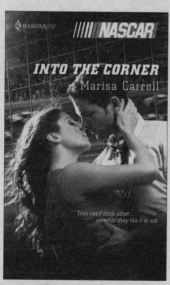

Love Inspired

SUSPENSE

RIVETING INSPIRATIONAL ROMANCE

PROTECTING *the* WITNESSES

*New identities, looming danger and forever love
in the Witness Protection Program.*

Cheyenne Rhodes has come to Redemption, Oklahoma, to start anew, not to make new friends. But single dad Trace Bowman isn't about to let her hide her heart away. He just needs to convince Cheyenne that Redemption is more than a place to hide—it's also a way to be found....

Look for

Finding Her Way Home

by

Linda Goodnight

REDEMPTION RIVER

Available January wherever books are sold.

www.SteepleHill.com

Steeple Hill®

LI87571

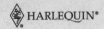
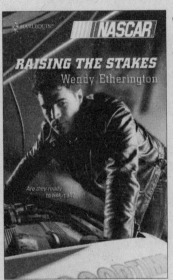